The Shopkeeper's Family

Finding a Path in the Dark of Night

The Shopkeeper's Family

Finding a Path in the Dark of Night

A Novel

E. N. Klinginsmith

Nyle Klinginsmith
11/1/2024

Compass Flower Press
Columbia, Missouri

Published by
Compass Flower Press
Columbia, Missouri

Library of Congress Control Number: 2024902880
ISBN: 978-1-951960-58-2 Trade Paperback
ISBN: 978-1-951960-59-9 Ebook

◈ Preface ◈

By the time I had breakfast with the man I'm calling George Mueller, a mutual friend had given me a piece George had written for his family—a story he called "A Backward Glance." While it was only sixteen pages, calling it a glance did it a disservice.

His story began in 1939 when, at the age of three, George and his family were forced by the Nazis to move from their German village in Romania to Germany. That move was followed by moves to Poland, Bohemia, Austria, and then to Germany again, with all of them made before George was ten and during one of the most tumultuous periods in world history. So "Glance," with its prose both concise and poetic, took me to all the places where George lived, while portraying the difficulties and dangers his family faced as they made their way through war-torn Europe.

Reading his story sparked an urge to bring it to a wider audience, so I asked the friend who'd shared it with me if he could arrange a meeting with George. I wanted to meet the man with that remarkable story, but more than that, I wanted to ask him if I could attempt to do something with it, knowing that he might be reluctant to give permission to a man he'd just met.

So when we met that morning, I told George I thought his narrative was a piece of history that needed to be shared beyond the small group of people who'd been privileged to see it. I asked him if he'd object to my trying to turn it into a book but without pushing him too hard. Instead, I gave him a novel I'd written. It was nothing great, but I hoped it was good enough to convince him I might be able to do his story justice. He read my book, and the next time we met, he agreed to let me give his story a try, but only if I wrote it as a novel, using different names to provide a level of privacy to his family.

I had pictured it as a biography and was a bit disappointed at first that it wouldn't be. Then as I thought about it, writing it as a novel was the only way it could be done, and it would allow me some artistic freedom I wouldn't have had otherwise. While his account was compelling, it needed dialog and minor characters to fill in gaps and provide plausible reasons for why certain events happened. I set about creating those people and events, while conducting research to add context and to ensure that matters such as policy, military history, and even simple things such as farming practices would be treated accurately.

And so we have come to *The Shopkeeper's Family*, a piece of historical fiction based on real events in the lives of the Mueller family, while using the times and places where they lived to provide its timeline. Some quotes are taken directly from "A Backward Glance" with George's permission. In other places, his words have been used but with slight changes to help with the flow of the story. The rest of the book is informed speculation as to how things might have happened, while keeping it as realistic as I could make it, these decades later and an ocean away from where it happened.

Nyle Klinginsmith
Columbia, Missouri
September 2023

✑ 1 ✑

Forced Departure

Late August 1939

The boat rolled slightly in the current, and there was commotion on the dock as the Mueller family waited amid the clamorous crowd. Finally, it was their turn to board, and they shuffled up the plank with friends just ahead of them and people they didn't know close behind.

The man at the top yelled, "Hurry up! Others need to board!"

The boy held on to his mother's dress. Johanna knew her three-year-old was terrified, and she wanted to hold him and reassure him it would be all right, but she couldn't. "Hold on tight, Georg. The ramp is narrow and my hands are full." His mother, father, sister, and brother were all loaded with bags and bundles stuffed with as many possessions as could be squeezed into them.

Herman led the way with Rolf at his side. Rolf was struggling with a burden that was all a boy of eight could carry, and Herman reached down to help with an item that was about to fall from the boy's bag. It was the family Bible, tied with string. This Bible was treasured because it held the family's handwritten genealogy going back to the days when the Mueller ancestors lived west of the Rhine, as well as a few precious pictures of their lives in Tariverde, Romania.

After he secured the book, Herman looked back to check on Johanna and the other children. Little Georg, his mother's dress still clutched tightly in his fist, smiled when he saw his father looking at him, and Herman tried his best to muster a smile in return. Annelise, ten and the oldest of the three, was to her mother's left, carrying as much as could be squeezed into an old leather case. The clothing belonged to her and her younger brothers, and even though those items had been carefully folded and stuffed into the case, there wasn't much there for any of them.

Two days earlier, as August turned to September, the Muellers—along with other Germanic families from their region—loaded into wagons and began the journey to the Romanian seaport city of Constanta. Johanna wanted desperately to bring more, but the wagon couldn't hold everything she wanted, and they'd been told by the German officials there'd be little room on the boat. "People will be the priority on the voyage, not possessions. Bring only what is essential and as little of that as you can."

As Herman looked at his wife, he saw her eyes were red from the tears she'd shed during a quiet moment on the road when she thought no one was watching. When Johanna looked back at her husband, his face mirrored hers, with the same sense of loss of nearly everything they'd owned, of their way of life, of hope for the future, and of any sense of control they'd ever allowed themselves to feel.

When the Muellers made it to the top of the ramp, they stepped onto the boat's deck. This boat would soon take its passengers up the Danube to an uncertain future in Germany. War was coming to Europe, and men in leadership roles had already begun hatching plans, drawing lines on maps, brokering deals, and launching campaigns that would lay waste to Europe and shatter the lives of millions of its people. Ordering villagers to board that boat was merely one of those arrangements. It mattered little to the Nazis that few of those families had ever lived in Germany. In fact, when most of their ancestors left there, it was a collection of small states and still more than a century away from becoming a country.

But by that late-August day, a now-unified Germany had already annexed the Sudetenland and Austria, established a rump government in Bohemia and Moravia, and signed an agreement allowing the Nazis to use military force to take possession of much of Poland. Additional moves were already planned, and the Nazis had determined it was imperative to bring people of German blood back to the Fatherland. Factories, farms, and the Wehrmacht would need people, and any territory overtaken by German armies would need German families to move there to provide the Lebensraum Hitler desired.

As the families of Tariverde boarded the boat for their trip up the Danube, some of the children were excited by it all. The boat was bigger than anything they had ever seen, and sailing up the river seemed to be a great adventure. For the adults, however, there would be no pleasure in this voyage. All of them had been born in Romania and spent their lives there, so it was there—especially the region known to them as Dobrogea that was home more than any place in Germany could ever be.

Once on board, the families were directed to go below deck and find a space in the crush of people. The boat would soon begin to work its way up the Danube. At the end of that journey, the descendants of Anton and Luise Mueller, a couple who'd left the village of Altenbamberg more than 150 years earlier, would be back in Germany. Unlike Anton, whose departure had been a matter of choosing the promise of a better life, Herman and Johanna were given no choice. They could either comply or face a life that promised poverty, imprisonment, and perhaps death.

∽ 2 ∾

Altenbamberg, Rhineland-Palatinate

1783

"Come with us, Anton! There's nothing here for us but hard work with little to show for it. There is promise of a better life in *Galizien*. We'll have our own land and plenty of it. We can make a future for our children and for theirs."

Anton Mueller was surrounded by a crowd urging him and his family to join them in a move that would forever change their lives. His head turned from person to person, following the voices. Finally, he raised his palm to quiet them. "So what is it we know of this new land, this Galizien?"

His friend Ernst answered, "It is part of Austria now. We know there is plenty of land to be farmed and they want us there." Another spoke up. "And we'll be free. There are rumors that there will be no taxes and no military obligations to Her Majesty Maria Theresa. We'll move there, take over the land, and bring civilization to that backwards country."

Anton, his lips pursed and his brow wrinkled, said, "I don't know. I've learned that when things seem too good to be true . . ."

A third man shouted, "Then stay here if you will! No one is forcing you!"

Ernst, more of a friend to Anton than the last man, said, "We want you to come. If we all go there, it will seem like home."

Anton hesitated. "I don't know. My wife is worried for our three children."

The other man shouted, "Who is the man of your house?"

That irritated Anton. "Step closer, Klaus, and allow me to show you who the man is here!"

Ernst intervened, getting between the two and glaring at the unfriendly man. "He should talk to his wife, Klaus, you know that." Then he turned back to Anton. "But to convince her, you only need to remind her how hard it is here and that it won't be any better for our children." Then, poking Anton in the chest for emphasis, Ernst continued, "For your three children, when they grow up. None of us have much here, and what little we have will be nothing when it's divided among our children."

Anton knew he was right. "This is true. Okay, I'll talk with her. When do you leave?"

"We leave next month. You need to be with us."

Although he knew Ernst was right, Luise wouldn't be easy to convince.

———————

Weeks later, they walked through the village of Altenbamberg for the final time. Anton carried their youngest cradled in his left arm, with his right arm around his wife's shoulders. The two older children walked in front of them. The Muellers said a final farewell to friends and family who were staying behind. Other farewells happened throughout the village that evening. Unspoken during those goodbyes was the certainty that those who were leaving would never again see the ones left behind. There was a torrent of tears that night, and there wasn't a single home in Altenbamberg where people slept well.

At sunup, the wagons started eastward. The distance was nearly nine hundred kilometers, and it would take several weeks to get there.

———————

The road was difficult, and even though Anton and the other men did their best, there was no way to avoid all the ruts and the rough patches. They wanted to make good time, but wagons loaded with family and belongings were slow-going for the teams of horses. The children, who'd been excited at first, cried and complained. Luise, never completely convinced the move was the thing to do, had gone silent during long stretches. Anton knew she was homesick, and even though he tried not to show it, he was as well.

Anton guided the team, navigating the rough road, looking for the smoothest route. He was ready to be done with the journey, ready to start their new life, but it would still be several days before they made it to Galizien. At the camp one night, after days on the road, one family announced they were returning to Altenbamberg, but the others talked them out of it. They convinced the family that traveling all that way alone would put them at risk of bandits, and nothing would have changed to make their prospects any better if and when they did make it home.

When he reached his low points—times when he also thought of returning—Anton reminded himself of the promises made by Maria Theresa, and he hoped those promises wouldn't be empty ones.

Finally, after two months on the road, they made it to their new homes near the town of Brigidau in what is today Ukraine. They saw few homes on the land, and those they saw were not in good shape, and that could have been a clue had they paid attention. While some of the land was good, much of it was marshy and unfit for agriculture. When they pulled up to their property and Anton and Luise saw it for the first time, he said little, but she cried, "What have we done, Anton?"

Anton, the head of this family and the man who'd brought them there, felt he needed to show optimism. "It will take some work, but we will make this our home, and if we treat it well, it will provide for us."

And so, that summer of 1783 the men set about building shelters for their families while they planted what they could. That done, they started to work on drainage ditches to dry out the topsoil and create more acreage to farm. There was no machinery, and most of the work had to be done by hand. To make matters worse, small ditches wouldn't drain enough water to make a difference. The topsoil was still marshy and nearly impossible to work. The ditches required walls higher than a man's head to be effective.

Anton Mueller wasn't afraid of work. Day after day he dug. He tried different methods and compared notes with other men. For him, the best approach was to dig a long, shallow trench, a shovelful of dirt at a time. He'd throw it to the side, then he would return and deepen the trench, not to its final depth, but deeper than before, and repeat until the walls were too high for that approach. When it got to that point, he made a wooden sled to drag the dirt to the end of the ditch where his horses waited at the top. He'd attach a long rope to the hitch and have his horses pull the heavy load up a ramp. The water kept pouring in as he worked, making digging and dredging slow and difficult.

He kept at it—digging, draining the land, and adding more acreage to the farm until a fateful day when he'd finished his normal morning chores.

He opened the door and yelled at Luise that he was taking the horses to the field to finish work on a ditch. She called back to him and told him she'd see him that evening.

He made it to the ditch then sang a favorite tune from his childhood as he backed the team of horses to the top of the trench. That done, he took his shovel and made his way down the ramp. He slogged through the muck, thankful that on the warmest days of summer there wasn't as much of it. He went to work, removing shovelfuls of dirt at the base of a high wall, mere meters from the ramp. He was excited, because he knew when he reached that ramp, he would be finished with this trench. As he pulled the shovelful of mud away from the wall and prepared to dump it in the sled, the sodden wall in front of him started to cave in, followed unexpectedly by the dirt on the two side walls. It was slow at first, but enough to catch his feet and render him unable to move. Then the walls, having been compromised, gave way and knocked him down. More dirt came, followed by still more, and he was soon buried. He fought to free himself, but the weight of it was too much, and it kept coming.

———

When the sun had started to set, and Anton hadn't returned, Luise sensed something was wrong. She sent their youngest son to fetch their neighbor Ernst. He came astride his horse with her son behind him. Ernst looked at Luise, and as she stood there with a new baby on her hip, his heart sank. He told her he was sure Anton was just having trouble with his horses or he wanted to finish the trench before he returned. He promised her he would be back soon with Anton at his side. Luise smiled, wanting to believe him. The boy slid off, and Luise directed Ernst to where her husband had been working.

The sun was nearing the horizon as Ernst approached the spot, and there, silhouetted against the sky, were Anton's two horses, waiting for their owner to come out of the ditch and take them home. Ernst whistled and yelled for Anton, but he heard nothing in return. When he made it to the ditch, he was horrified at the sight. There at the bottom of the ditch, the dirt had caved in, and only the tip of a shovel's handle showed above. He knew his friend was dead, but he went into the ditch and clawed at the mud until he uncovered Anton's hand. It was cold and lifeless, and he knew he'd lost his friend. He thought back to the day in Altenbamberg when he had led the crowd in convincing Anton to come with them, and he cried out, "What have I done to you, Anton?"

Ernst crawled out of the ditch and took his horse by the reins. He got control of Anton's team and walked the three horses to the house, where Luise and the children stood in the yard. He could see the hope in her eyes at first, but when he walked toward her leading the horses, she knew her Anton was dead.

"He's gone, Luise, buried by the walls of the ditch. In the morning, I'll get some help and we'll bring him home."

Luise slumped to the ground and gathered her children to her. They were unsure at first, but soon they could tell by their mother's sobs, they'd lost their father. The cries of the children joined their mother's, and Ernst could only stand there, grief-stricken himself and uncertain what he should do. Then as every practical German would, he took the horses to their stall, unhitched them, and gave them water and oats. When he emerged, Luise was standing, with tears still streaming down her cheeks, but quieter now. Ernst went to her and held her against him as she cried yet again for her Anton. Ernst knew he had two families to care for now, but he was sure others would help as well.

Anton Mueller left Luise with four children, including the baby who'd been born after they'd settled near Brigidau. She had to deal with the shock of her husband's death and the dilemma of what to do now that she was head of the household. In the days that followed, she considered loading her family into the wagon to make the long trek back to Altenbamberg, but just as it hadn't been an option for the family on the road a few years before, it wasn't for hers. If they made it, they'd be homeless, with only a few pfennigs to their name. In Brigidau at least they had a home, so for the time being, Brigidau was where they'd stay. And with the help of Ernst, along with their neighbors and friends, they were able to continue. In fact, four more generations of Muellers made Brigidau their home. They survived there, but never prospered, and on the most difficult days they wondered if a better life might be found elsewhere.

———

That opportunity came in 1886, a short time after the region of Northern Dobrogea became part of Romania, a new nation emerging from years of control by the Ottoman Turks. Some families from German states had already settled there while it was still under Ottoman rule. When the region became part of Romania, the settlers were joined by others from Germany and from places under Russian control.

When Gerhard Mueller heard about the opportunity nearly 2,000 kilometers to the south of them, he was unsure at first. It could never be as good as his friends and neighbors made it out to be. But like them, he was tired of the hard life in Galicia and weary of its long, unrelenting winters.

"It's warmer there," they said. "The soil is better. Other Germans are moving there, so we'll live among people like us." The talk was reminiscent of the arguments used to persuade Anton and Luise to move. Unlike Luise Mueller, Gerhard's wife favored this move, thinking it could provide a better life for them and their children. Eventually she prevailed, and just a little over a century after his great-great-grandfather Anton had moved his family to Brigidau, Gerhard Mueller moved his family south.

They made their way to Tariverde, a farming community located in Constanta, a county near the Black Sea. The first task upon arrival was to build shelter for their families, but shelter was useless without water, so they began to dig wells. As was the case with the ditches, well-digging was a dangerous enterprise, and men lost their lives in the process. The method used for excavating called for the well-diggers to wait until they finished the entire well before reinforcing its walls, and this often resulted in a collapse. If a man was at the bottom when that happened, he was trapped, and if enough dirt came down, there was no air to breathe and death soon would follow. Finally, some wise person figured out a way to shore the walls as the men dug, and men no longer died trying to provide water for their families. With shelter in place and water secured, they had more time for farming and other means of livelihood. The village of Tariverde became one of several thriving Germanic enclaves in the delta region of the Danube, and life was good.

❦ 3 ❧

Georg Mueller

1936

Tariverde was a planned community. The farm yards were all the same width and depth. In front of the houses there was a gravel road, a ditch, a green space, another ditch, a gravel road, and more farm yards. The yards were enclosed by masonry walls. All the yards were private. If Gypsies called any place home, it would be Romania. A few Romanians, Turks, and Ukrainians lived on the outskirts of the village, but most of the two thousand residents were German. We had German schools and a German church and [we] spoke German. The town had two blacksmiths, at least one shoemaker, and two carpenter shops. We had no doctors. Tariverde also had two general stores. My family owned one of them. On the edge of town there was a grain windmill owned by my uncle Peter. He also built an "oil windmill." It was an oil press operated by wind power to make oil from flax, rape, and poppy seeds. This windmill also turned an electric generator that produced light for both windmills. My uncle offered the town free electricity if they bought the wire themselves. There were no takers.

—Excerpt from "A Backward Glance"

Georg Mueller, grandson of Gerhard, was born in Tariverde on an unseasonably hot Sunday in April 1936. He was the third child of Herman and Johanna. Georg's sister, Annelise, was seven years old when he was born, and his brother, Rolf, was five.

Herman's store occupied the front of their house and was something of a focal point for the neighborhood. Georg loved to play there, and his father allowed it so long as he didn't interrupt conversations with customers or touch items for sale. He was often in trouble for doing both, including the day he spilled walnuts all over the floor while trying to lay his hands on a pocketknife his father had on display. His father and a customer were engaged in conversation when the clatter of dozens of walnuts hitting the floor interrupted them. Herman grew quiet, then said, "You will pick those up, Son!"

Georg worshipped his father, and all it took was a raised voice or a disapproving look to reduce him to tears. As those tears began, Herman leaned down, picked up the basket, and handed it to Georg. "There's no need for tears, just pick them up and it will be okay."

The boy sniffled as he began gathering the nuts, which by that time had scattered far and wide, finding places to hide that only a boy on his hands and knees could see. When he'd finished and the customer had left, his father said, "If you wanted a nut, you should have just asked. I would have let you have one."

The boy sheepishly told his father it wasn't a nut he wanted but one of the knives.

"You are much too young to be handling one of those!"

The tears returned.

His father kneeled to be at eye level with the boy and said, "But when you are older, I will see that you have a nice one."

Georg broke into a big smile. He'd been promised a pocketknife and given a wonderful memory of his father.

The Mueller house sat at the right side of a good-sized yard. There was a well on one side, and behind the house, an outhouse and a root cellar. At the back of the property, there were stalls for the horses, cows, and pigs. There was also a chicken house and a large garden plot that provided vegetables and root crops to go along with the eggs, milk, and meat from their animals.

The other houses in Tariverde were similar in design to the Muellers', although there were slight differences based on the financial well-being of the families. While the Muellers were relatively prosperous, the Schusters— the family across the street—were a poor but proud bunch. The father was a shoemaker, and he and his wife had seven children, all boys. Georg played with the boys so often, it was said he was the Schusters' eighth son.

There were times the Schusters had very little food to eat and resorted to catching the starlings that nested in the reed roof of their house. Georg remembers eating with the Schusters and cleaning the bones of the birds. As hard as times got for them, the Schusters never asked for, nor accepted, charity from their neighbors. Years later, Georg learned that all seven boys had become doctors or engineers.

The houses were separated by the ditches, green space, and roads found throughout the village. The buffer provided some semblance of protection from roving bands who lived on the outskirts of Tariverde and coveted what the German villagers had. For the Muellers, their two dogs completed the security system. One of the dogs was chained to a runner that allowed him to go from the front gate to the well in the side yard. The other was chained in the same fashion in the back yard. The dogs were pets to the family but huge and menacing to strangers.

ⅎ **4** ⅏

War and the *Auslandsdeutsche* of Tariverde

1939

> I was three and a half years old when we left Tariverde, so some of this may be suggestive memories, but I do remember playing with a little red fire car with pedals. I don't recall how well it worked on gravel. I remember picking chamomile on top of the root cellar, the church bell ringing and the steeple swaying from an earthquake. I remember glass shards embedded in the masonry wall in the rear of the yard . . . and the time a plane flew over and people were jumping and pointing at it. I recall just little snippets of memory for a time long gone.

—Excerpt from "A Backward Glance"

The men who came from Germany and brought an end to this happy time were most likely part of VoMi, the German acronym for the Main Welfare Office for Ethnic Germans, a division that later became part of the SS. Perhaps they came to each home in Tariverde to deliver the edict, or maybe it was delivered to all the men of the town at some mandated meeting. However it was done, those men from VoMi reminded the villagers that they were of German heritage, and German blood flowed in their veins. The situation in Europe made it necessary for Germans living abroad to return to their homeland.

To entice the Tariverdians to come home, the uniformed men appealed to their sense of patriotism and made promises of housing and jobs. The villagers' responses to those appeals and promises ranged from indifference to resistance, so the men from VoMi let the villagers know that an agreement with the Romanians had already been reached, and the move would happen.

The families of Tariverde, like other German families in Dobrogea and throughout the Balkans, were expected to leave their homes and come home to the Reich.

When Herman delivered this news to Johanna, she was distraught. "We're people of Dobrogea as much as we're Germans. We've never lived there. What's going on in Germany is none of our concern. Why can't we stay, Herman?"

"I'm not sure. They seem determined to have us leave, and the Romanians are cooperating with them, and if that is the case, then . . ."

"Can we hold off with this decision? Maybe if enough of us resist, we can stay. This life is all we know, Herman. Tariverde is our home. Let's not give up."

Herman looked lovingly at his wife. He understood and felt every word of what she was saying. He promised her he'd talk with the other men of the village to see if they would join in resisting the demands of the agents of the Nazis. Maybe if there was a unified response, then the deal would be called off and they could stay.

The next day, the store was busier than usual, with people stopping by to talk with Herman and with each other. Some vowed they wouldn't be forced out. Others showed doubt, worried that a few families had already left and others would soon follow. There was resignation in those voices.

Herman listened and encouraged. He reassured people that he and Johanna had no intention to leave; they were determined to stay in their house and run the store for years into the future, no matter what was going on in Germany and the rest of Europe.

His strong words lifted spirits and renewed determination among the listeners. This resolve lasted longer with some than with others. For a few, it faded almost as soon as they left his store. It had to last with Herman though, because he knew his wife was determined to stay.

At one point in the late afternoon, Herman's brother, Peter, came in to talk with him. "What do you think of all this, Herman?"

"It's worrisome for sure. I've been talking with people all day, and some are on the verge of doing as we've been told by VoMi. Others are still strong, and they're determined to stay." He looked at his brother. "So what do you think, Peter?"

"My wife and I talked late last night after the boys were asleep. We're starting to think we may have to leave Tariverde. We may have no choice but to go to Germany."

"Why leave? If we stand together, they can't make us go."

"But they'll pick the weak ones off, and soon the tide will turn against us."

"That's how they want us to think, Peter."

Peter took a deep breath before continuing. "You know the Romanians don't like us, and they'll ally with the Germans to make sure we leave."

"I'm aware they aren't fond of us. But I've seen no animosity. Why would they join the Germans in this?"

"First, we've kept in our own little world here, never really becoming a part of Romania. They see us as strangers who speak another language and keep apart from them."

"I ask you, is that enough for them to want us to leave? We don't harm them. We do business with them. We aren't their enemies, nor are they ours."

"No, but we're more strangers than friends, you see, and they look at what we've built here and resent and envy us."

"Still, that doesn't seem enough for them to join the Germans in expelling us."

"It's the oil, Herman."

"The oil?"

"We're being traded for oil. The word is there is very little good oil in Germany, and certainly not enough for a country growing as it is now. Germany needs oil for its factories and vehicles, and based on what we are hearing these past few weeks, for its army as well. Romania has oil, lots of it and of far better quality, and Germany is more than willing to pay for it. The word is that Romania has already agreed to the sale, but the Germans are required to take us back to complete their part of the bargain. Yes, they tell us we're countrymen to them, and they think all people of German heritage should come home. And yes, we can assume they need us to work in their factories, and God help us, they may need us and our sons in their armies too. But at the end of it all, I think this is about the oil as much as it is about all of that."

"I see."

"So we must think about leaving. It's a wise man who considers this and makes plans for the welfare of his family."

"I'll think about it, and I'll consider such plans, but I'm not giving up yet."

Peter left at that point, but the conversation bothered Herman, and he spoke with Johanna about it that night. They knew that if they gave in, it would be a turning point, because other families looked to them as a source of strength and hope.

Herman tried to put on a brave face as the people came through the next day, but it was difficult. He listened more than he talked. The prevailing mood of the villagers was to stay, hoping the men would give up.

Perhaps someone from VoMi witnessed all the activity in the store and concluded that Herman Mueller was a person of influence in the community. Some action was needed to encourage him to leave Tariverde, because if he agreed to move, others would soon follow.

The next morning when Herman went outside, the two dogs were gone. Their collars had been cut, their chains were on the ground, and they were nowhere to be found. He went back in the house to tell Johanna and to see if she'd heard anything unusual during the night. She told him that while she didn't sleep well, she wasn't aware of anything out of the ordinary. The dogs might have barked once or twice, but that wasn't unusual. They often barked at imagined noises or even at the moon.

Johanna was shocked to think someone had taken their pets. The intruders must have made some noise. The dogs surely had to bark and raise a ruckus. How could she not have heard? How could someone slip in and take their protectors like that? Herman suggested the thieves might have been people the dogs knew and trusted, but that seemed unlikely. No person they knew would have taken their dogs.

Herman went back outside to get some water from the well, and when he reached it he could tell its cover had been tampered with. He dreaded what he might see if he removed that cover. He slowly slid the two wooden pieces aside and tried to peer down into the well's shaft, but the sun wasn't high enough for him to see all the way to the water, so he went inside to get a lantern.

"Why do you need a lantern in the morning, Herman?"

"Something isn't right at our well. I need to look inside it."

Herman wore a look Johanna had seldom seen in all their years of marriage, and it worried her. She was sure it had to do with the dogs, and she began to consider something so horrible it sickened her.

"I'll come with you."

"You don't have to do that. It might be bad."

"No, I'm coming."

The children were just stirring, so she ordered them to stay inside until she came back. Even little Georg could tell it was no time to disobey.

When they reached the well, Herman tied a short rope to the lantern's handle and lowered it a few feet down the shaft. When the light was just right, they could see their beloved dogs' bodies wedged against each other in the well, poisoned most likely, and left there as a warning.

Herman cursed as Johanna gasped and covered her mouth. Herman slid the covers over the well, knowing that somehow he would have to rig a way to retrieve the bodies of their dogs from the deep well shaft. Certainly his family wouldn't be able to drink its water now, nor would they be able to for a long time. He wondered if the well would have to be filled up and sealed, and a new one dug—a long and costly procedure. They could borrow small amounts of water from the neighbors each day, maybe enough to get by, but the worry of something worse took hold. These were terrible people who had killed their dogs. Would his resistance put his wife and children at risk? Was there any choice left to him?

Herman and Johanna stood there for a moment trying to process what had happened and think about what to do next. Then the question of how to tell the children arose. Certainly the three would notice their big, beloved dogs missing.

"Can we tell them the Gypsies did this, Herman?"

"For now, yes."

When they told the children about the missing dogs and explained why they would have to go to the neighbors to get buckets of water for the time being, Georg wasn't old enough to truly understand, but Rolf and Annelise were grief-stricken at the loss of Samson and Maximillian. They could remember the dogs coming to them as playful puppies. They'd watched them grow as they themselves had grown. To learn that their dogs had been killed was almost too much for them, and they hated the Gypsies for it. Herman and Johanna felt guilty for being dishonest, but better that the children feel anger toward the Gypsies than know the awful truth. The time to tell it might come—would come most likely, but that wasn't the day for it.

———

That night, after the children were asleep, Herman and Johanna sat quietly at the kitchen table and talked about the day.

"What will we do, Herman?"

"I think we'll have to leave. The kind of people who did what these people have done..." He hesitated, choosing his words carefully. "I think that people like that, nothing will stop. If we stay, you and our children are in danger. No good husband, no loving father can allow that."

"So . . . how do we do this?"

"I'll talk to the authorities tomorrow and negotiate the move."

Johanna looked around at their home. She could see an end coming to what they knew. The tears began, quietly at first, turning into sobs as Herman held her, shedding tears himself. Annelise was awakened by the noise and crept to the kitchen door. She peeked through the narrow opening, saw her parents holding each other, and heard her mother weeping. Annelise caught just enough of the conversation to know her parents were making plans to leave Tariverde. Before that day her friends had talked of the men who'd come to the village telling the families they would be moved to Germany, but Annelise had chosen not to believe those friends. On that awful night, she could no longer pretend a move would never happen. She returned to her bed, where like her parents, Annelise shed tears while her younger brothers slept. She said a silent prayer that some miracle would happen and it would all be a dream. She had trouble going to sleep that night and when she did, she dreamed of dogs in the well and men coming into their village, ordering them to leave.

———

When Annelise came to the table the next morning, her mother noticed she was quiet. Rolf, still in shock over losing the dogs, was barely more talkative than his sister. Georg babbled a bit, but soon he too grew quiet.

"Children, eat your breakfast. It's good bread I've made, and you love the jam, and there's a bit of ham from last night too. It's good. Don't waste it."

The boys did as their mother instructed, while Annelise picked at her food. Johanna guessed there was something to her quiet demeanor, and she studied her daughter to see what it might be. Finally, the girl looked up at her mother, and in that moment Johanna could tell her ten-year-old daughter had pieced things together.

"Boys, we need water. Please take two buckets and get some from the Schusters. Rolf, help your brother if his bucket gets too heavy."

The boys finished their breakfast and left to get the water, and Johanna sat down beside her daughter. She took Annelise's two hands in hers. "It will be all right. Whatever happens, we'll be together."

She said, "I know, Mother." Her tears started again, and her mother pulled her close. While Johanna hated what all this was doing to her and Herman, she hated even worse the uncertain future facing Annelise and her brothers.

Johanna didn't let Annelise know that Herman had gone first to tell his brother of their plans, then to arrange passage for the family up the Danube. Herman was hoping the two families would go at the same time and to the same place. Herman felt a special bond with his older brother Peter, because it was Peter, twenty years older than he, who had taken responsibility and raised him when their parents died. Herman was so young when it happened that he remembered little of his mother and father. Peter was as much of a father as Herman had ever had, and if they had to leave Tariverde, the Mueller brothers should be together.

From that day on, everything would be a blur. Word spread of the killing of the Muellers' dogs and of their decision to leave. In Tariverde and across the region, other families soon suffered similar fates and worse. The tide had turned, and within months more than thirteen thousand people of Germanic heritage would leave their homes in Dobrogea and be resettled in Germany, and among them would be the two Mueller brothers, their wives, and children.

⤳ 5 ⤶

The Danube and the Convent

Fall 1942

Three years later, on a fall afternoon, Georg was sitting at the kitchen table enjoying a slice of his mother's bread. She put another loaf in the oven, then came to sit by him.

"How was school today, Georg?"

"It was okay."

"And your new teacher? Do you like her?"

"She's all right."

Johanna smiled, because that was high praise coming from Georg.

"Mother?"

"Yes?"

"Some older kids were talking about the time they were on a boat, and I remembered we were on one too. Do you think it could have been the same one?"

"Oh, Georg. I doubt it; there were hundreds of them that fall."

"I don't remember a lot about it."

"You were only three. It's not surprising."

"Can you tell me?"

"I'm not sure what I would want to tell you. The boat trip was anything but enjoyable." She paused, memories returning, and she sorted through them, considering if there were any she wished to share. "I suppose I can tell you, but before I do, maybe you should tell me what you remember."

He took another bite of his bread, and like every boy of six, he answered with his mouth full. "I remember we were all in one big room, so it was crowded, and I remember we had only bunk beds, and it smelled bad."

"You remember more than you think." She paused. It was unpleasant to think about it and even more so to talk about it, but he'd asked. "When we made it to Constanta, we were loaded onto a boat that was meant for freight and not for people. You know the difference?"

27

He thought he might, but he wasn't sure.

"It means it didn't have cabins or rooms for passengers, just a big hold where we all had to sleep."

"So why did they put us on such boats?"

"The men who'd forced us to move wanted to get as many of us up the river and into Germany as soon as they could, so they used every boat that was available. They even paid some Romanians to use their boats to help."

"Was our boat Romanian?"

"No, ours was German. It might have been better than a Romanian boat, but not much I would guess."

Johanna grew quiet as she thought of the cramped conditions, the darkness, the noise, the smells, and the worry of it all. She remembered that the women and young children were separated from the men and older boys, and that she had to drape sheets over the bunk beds so they had some privacy when changing clothes.

There were a few good times, such as when they were allowed on deck, where they stood watching the passing countryside as the old boat plied its way up the Danube. There was one occasion when the boat pulled in to replenish supplies and take on fuel. When it docked, she looked longingly at the town. She would have given anything to disembark and walk its streets, if for no other reason than to breathe air that didn't reek of other people and diesel fumes. But the German men who promised them such a bright future forbade the passengers from leaving. The irony of that did not go unnoticed.

The trip grew long, and as the days passed, she and Herman began to talk about what might happen when they reached Germany. They knew there was no going back, so they began to think how they'd provide for their children and ensure their safety once they left the boat. It wasn't as if they were excited about the next chapter, but they'd grown weary of being on the boat and were ready to exchange worries about the unknown for whatever challenges might await them. Then word came from the crew that they were sailing through Germany, and would soon be leaving the boat.

"Mother?"

"Oh Georg, I'm sorry. You got me thinking about the boat and our time in Löhr. Please go ahead and ask me any questions you still have."

He looked at her. He enjoyed being in the kitchen with her, smelling the bread in the oven and dinner cooking on the stove. Annelise was away at school in Prague, and Rolf was helping Herman with some fence that needed repair. Georg finished his bread, then said, "I remember the day we left the boat."

"You do?"

"Yes, I remember they put us in the back of a truck with some other families."

She was amazed he remembered that, but then it was a day not easily forgotten. They were ushered off the boat in the same rude fashion they'd boarded it, and then they were escorted to the convent by a local functionary. The man said very little when he greeted them at the dock—something to the effect of, "You're here. We'll take you to your new residence and get you settled today. You may see your new village later." Not every family on the boat was sent to Löhr. Other families were taken to other places. There was sadness at the parting, and they made assurances they would stay in touch. Times and situations would prove to make that difficult, but not impossible.

As if he was reading his mother's mind, he asked, "And that was when Uncle Peter's family left us?"

"Yes. They were sent to Frankfurt."

"I have trouble remembering what they looked like. Do you think we'll get to see them again sometime?"

Johanna didn't answer at first. They'd had news from Peter that wasn't good, so she chose her words carefully. "I hope so, but they're having a hard time right now, and it's not a good time for them to travel, and we can't leave the farm to go see them."

He took one more bite of bread, chewing it as his young mind went back to work. "I remember the convent."

"You do?"

"It seemed like the boat in some ways. It was big and there were so many of us, but at least we had a yard to play in."

"Yes, you did, and we had to chase you children out of our garden more than a few times."

Georg grinned. "When you grown-ups yelled at us we didn't pay too much attention. We were too busy playing."

"Watching you play was one of the good things about the convent."

"But there were times I got tired of all the other people. I wanted it to just be us."

"We all felt that way."

He finished his bread, and she could tell he'd had enough of the conversation. "Georg, I've talked too long, and there are things that need to be done. It's still light outside. Go outside and find your friend to play with."

"Okay, Mother."

She watched him leave, then got up to check on the bread that had been baking while they talked. As she checked it, her mind returned to those days in Löhr. It still amazed her that they had lived in that crowded convent for two years. They knew they would eventually be assigned a place to live, and Herman checked frequently with the authorities to see if there was news, ever mindful to avoid being a nuisance as he did. Those in charge might not take kindly to his hounding them, and they might punish his impudence by giving his family a horrible placement. Worse than that, his questions might draw attention to the fact that he was a healthy man in his thirties who needed something to do, and such a man could be pressed into the service of the Wehrmacht.

Some families left the convent, including a few friends who were sent to Czechoslovakia, a country with a sizable German population. As they left, others arrived to take their places, and still the Muellers waited. As the tide of Romanian-Germans grew, thousands were sent to Poland, including, in the late summer of 1941, the family of Herman and Johanna Mueller.

Thoughts of winter in Poland brought a chill to Johanna, even as she felt the heat coming from the oven.

$\backsim$ **6** $\rightsquigarrow$

Poland

1941

When Herman received the news that his family would be relocated to a farm in central Poland near Warthbrücken—called Koło by the Polish—he was anything but optimistic. Still, he tried to show a brave face when the time came to tell Johanna about it.

"Poland?"

"Yes, dear."

"But why there? Is there nothing for us here in Germany?"

"Apparently not. For others, yes, but not for us. If it helps, we won't be the only ones to be sent to Poland. They've told me that thousands of us are being sent there."

Johanna started to ask where all these thousands would be housed, then realized what the answer would be. Polish families had been forced to leave their homes, and those same homes would be the ones made available to the displaced German families.

When she considered this, she couldn't help but think back to what had happened in Tariverde. She knew some Romanian or Ukrainian family was living in their home in Tariverde by then, and the thought brought strong feelings of dismay. How could a person be happy to move to the former home of some poor Polish family who'd been forced to leave by the same Nazis who'd made the Muellers leave their home in Tariverde? While she knew their situation was better than those Polish families who didn't have the "benefit" of German ancestry, she felt no joy in that thought.

Herman seemed willing to accept this arrangement if it gave his family a place to live somewhere other than an overcrowded convent, with nothing to call their own. Johanna tried to set her thoughts, her guilt, and her resentment aside, but still she had questions. "What will we do in Poland, Herman? How will we make our living there?"

"We know how to grow things. There will be sugar beets and other root crops. We'll have animals to help us with the work and to help keep us fed."

"Your mind is made up on this?"

"We'll no longer be allowed to stay here in this convent. What choice do we have?"

Johanna looked around again, much as she had done in their home in Tariverde two years earlier. The conditions at the convent had been Spartan at best, and there was never a moment of privacy, but at least she knew what to expect there, and they were in a lovely village. She put forth her last argument: "Can we not leave and move to another place here in Germany? There must be work for you."

"Where would we go to find it? Who would we ask? Where would we live? How would we feed our three while I look for work?"

"It's nearly autumn, and they're sending us to Poland! It can't be much better there!"

"I've been promised that the officials in the region will provide for families like ours, just as they did here. They'll make sure we make it through the winter, and then we can provide for ourselves."

When spring comes, we'll plant our garden. We will fix up the house and make it our home. You'll see, Johanna, soon it will feel much like our old life, I promise."

Johanna grew quiet, then looked at her husband, just as he had looked at her a few moments earlier. He too had aged in the past years, but where her face showed worry, his wore a look of determination—still there after all they'd been through.

"Can we do this, Herman?"

"We'll have to."

Johanna wanted to believe that as much as he seemed to, but her doubts remained. *Perhaps the Polish countryside will be beautiful, and maybe there'll be enough others like us to make it feel like home again. And in the end, as Herman has just said, what other choice have we been given? We have children to take care of, and our children must always be our first concern.*

———

As they made their way to Poland in the summer of 1941, the German army was moving east as well. The peace with the Soviet Union ended in June with the launch of Operation Barbarossa. Germany was moving on Leningrad and Moscow and the coveted oil fields of the Crimea. The news was full of stories of glorious victories. The Muellers didn't join in celebrating those victories, but the thought that the border of Germany was now far east of where they would live provided some sense of security. There was also the hope that, given the successes, the Russians would surrender and there would be an end to the fighting. Life could go on, and if Johanna and Herman did their best to make a go of it in Poland, then other, better choices would come their way.

As they came to the farm, it looked uninviting, but not horrible. Looking at it from the road, there was a nice pond to the left of the yard with a barn to the left of that. Behind the barn there was a woodshed for firewood, a chicken coop, and fenced-in lots for the animals. The house was small and simple, sitting near the road and to the right as they looked at the property. It wasn't much of a house, and not nearly as nice as their old home. Beyond it, at the very back of the property, was a plot with turnips ready to be dug for winter.

Johanna set to work over the next weeks trying to make the house her own, although with its history it would never truly be. Herman dug the turnips and busied himself repairing fences and taking care of the farm's livestock and poultry.

Five-year-old Georg was too young for school, and with no German school nearby, Rolf and Annelise were sent to a school in a big city. The school was too far from home for a daily trip, so they had to board there. Neither of them was happy with the arrangement. On the day their parents left the two of them, Annelise cried and Rolf spoke angrily to his father. The trip back to their new home was a sad one for Herman and Johanna, and even for little Georg, who was already missing his siblings. When they made it back to their small house, it seemed quiet and empty and even less like home than before.

Georg was given a bicycle, and was excited to ride it into the village, even if he was unhappy that it was a full-sized women's bike that required him to stand on the pedals. To solve this problem, his father adapted the seat so it sat lower on the frame and his feet could reach the pedals. It was an improvement, but sitting lower meant he could barely see over the handlebars. Still, it offered him transportation and freedom and something to fill his time with Annelise and Rolf away at school.

Even with all Johanna's hard work, the house still lacked basic comforts. It had a dirt floor and a fireplace in the middle that provided only a little protection against the bitter cold of the Polish winter. There was a small kitchen but no summer kitchen, and there were only two bedrooms, so the children had to share when all three were home.

There were nights Johanna had trouble sleeping, and she thought she could hear the whispers and cries of those who'd lived in the house before. Maybe it was the wind, but she felt sadness and loss. She hated those nights, and she hated their lives in the countryside near Warthbrücken.

Things got better when Johanna's parents, the Baurichters, came from their small home in the eastern part of Germany to visit. Grandfather Baurichter pitched in to help wherever he could. Grandmother helped around the house and spent evenings operating the family's spinning wheel in a dimly lit corner of the room.

The spinning wheel was essential to their way of life. The fiber for it came from sheep on the farm. Herman took care of shearing, but Johanna and her mother took care of the rest. All the impurities like straw, weeds, and woodchips had to be picked out. The wool was washed and sometimes dyed. Every fiber was run between the fingertips and fed into the spinning wheel, which turned the threads into yarn. The spinning wheel was operated by foot.

The women made all the cloth and clothing, except for clothes for church. They sewed all the pants, shirts, and coats. They knitted all the socks, stockings, sweaters, headgear, mittens, and scarves. The boys were easier to clothe than the girls, because the only attire for boys from early spring till late fall was a pair of linen shorts held up by a rubber band sewn in the top. If the boys were lucky, the shorts had a pocket. In summer the boys would go shirtless, and in winter they wore heavier shorts, a sweater, long knitted stockings held up by suspenders, and of course, shoes.

It was during their visit that Grandfather Baurichter showed a sense of humor. He was out doing chores, with little Georg "helping." In addition to sheep, there were horses, cattle, and chickens to tend. When Georg went in to where the cattle were, Grandfather thought it would be funny to lock him in for a bit, but he soon released the boy. They moved on to feed the horses, then the chickens, and Georg hatched a plan to return the favor. When his Opa went inside the chicken coop, Georg locked the door. He didn't let him out right away, and being a boy, he was soon distracted and forgot to release his prisoner.

It wasn't until Herman heard Grandfather Baurichter yelling for someone to come and let him out that he gained release. Georg's parents were furious and ready to punish him, but his grandfather explained that the boy was only doing to him what he'd done to Georg minutes before. When they heard that, his parents decided not to punish him. As the story got retold, it became more humorous to everyone, even Georg's parents.

When winter arrived, it was beyond cold, and the cold was unrelenting. They did the best they could to manage in the old drafty house, but there was no way to keep it warm during the day, much less the bitter nights. Every one of those nights, Herman would get up and throw more wood in the stove to keep the house from freezing by morning.

The reports of the war would have them believe the Germans had the Soviet army in retreat, while in truth the army was experiencing its first setbacks of the war in Russia. The German people weren't told of such things. In mid-December though, word reached them that the Americans had entered the war on the side of the British and French. Herman and Johanna talked about it one night when Georg was asleep in his bed.

"Johanna, this isn't good news. When you add the strength of the Americans to our enemies, they'll become a formidable force."

Johanna sighed. "There are so many German families in America, I thought they'd help keep America out of the war, at least I hoped so."

"Well, the Japanese *idioten* bombed their ships at Pearl Harbor, and the Americans had no choice."

"What a stupid thing to do! And they are supposedly our friends." The way she said friends indicated her dislike of Germany's Asian allies.

"Yes, but it was inevitable that the Americans would come in. They've already been helping the British, providing them with military supplies and other goods, and from reports, the Japanese have been quite successful in the Pacific, and that couldn't have been seen as a good thing in America."

"And now it seems that American soldiers will be coming to join the others?"

"We can only hope most of them will go to fight the Japanese. That should be their primary opponent. After all, it was they who attacked the Americans, not us. Still, the United States is a big country with lots of people, and Germany is allied with the Japanese. American soldiers will be coming our way too. They'll be a problem in the west when they come, and there's still the Russian problem to the east."

"What will happen then?"

"There's no way to know for sure, but with so many more soldiers lined up against Germany, there will be no quick victories now. We are in for a long war I believe, and who can say how it will go?"

Johanna grew quiet. She hated the war and had no love for the Nazis, but the thought of a German defeat and the worry of how it would be for her family if that happened was equally bad. "The only hope lies in peace."

Herman reached across the table and patted her hand. "Peace is always the hope."

She took hold of his hand. "Annelise and Rolf will be home for Christmas soon."

He smiled. "At least we'll have that."

∽ 7 ∾

The Winter and Czechoslovakia

February 1942

Winters in central Europe are often cold, but that winter was the worst. As the days went by, Herman and Johanna began to look for a way out. Herman had tried to make things work on the Polish farm, but when he thought about the coming spring and the growing season ahead, he had deep concerns. It might be years before he'd make enough money to do the things the house and farm needed, and even the most basic items for his family would be difficult to buy during those years. They'd get by, perhaps, but little more than that, and that wasn't the future he wanted for his family.

The previous summer, when he'd been told about coming to Poland, Herman wanted to believe he could make the farm a success. He had some doubts, but moving to the farm was a way to get out of convent life, which by then had become nearly unbearable. During the spell of good weather when they first arrived, things did seem better, and at least his family was living in its own home. Then came the brutal winter, with its unbearable and dangerous cold, and it drove hope from him with each passing day. To run out of fuel in such weather, even for a short time, would prove fatal. Food wasn't abundant, and they were careful with it, because it too could run out, and that would also be the end of them.

They knew people who had settled in Czechoslovakia, and when a couple let them know of an opportunity there, they acted quickly. Just as Gerhard Mueller had done three-quarters of a century earlier, Herman prepared to take his family south.

Their last night in Poland was the worst, and it was the thought of better days ahead that got them through it. All their belongings had been shipped, and the few blankets they had left were not nearly enough. They nearly froze that night sitting next to the fireplace.

As soon as the sun rose on another frigid Polish day, the Muellers began their journey. They made their way by train to Czechoslovakia, where they met their friend Ritter. Herr Ritter and his wife had lived for a brief time at the convent before being sent to the town of Melník. Once there, they made several friends in the German community, and among those friends was a nice couple who'd moved to the nearby village of Strednitz a short time before Ritter and his wife had settled in Melník. The man died in June, around the time the Muellers were making their way to Poland. His widow tried to run the farm without him but quickly realized it was too much for her. One day, when she encountered Ritter in the village, she shared that she'd be moving to live with relatives in Germany and told him she hoped some nice German family could take over the farm.

As luck would have it, a letter from Johanna had arrived that day. In that letter she revealed to Frau Ritter how miserable life was in Poland, but how determined they were to make it work. When his wife read the letter to him, Ritter began to see a solution to two problems. Their friends could be rescued from cold, desolate central Poland, and the widow Huber would have that good family to take over her farm.

Ritter let Frau Huber know he had a possible replacement, and his wife immediately wrote to Johanna and informed her that a nice farm was available—one she was sure the Muellers would love. Frau Ritter assured Johanna that her husband would have no trouble arranging with local officials for the transfer of the property. He knew who to talk to and how to make things work.

The Muellers only had to hear of the opportunity to agree, and they gave Ritter the go-ahead to proceed with the transfer. The widow Huber was overjoyed at the news, and within a couple of weeks, she left for Germany. After her departure, Ritter made frequent trips to the farm to work with the three Czech families who lived and worked on the estate. The more he visited the place and got to know the people there, the more he knew he'd found the Muellers a perfect home.

———

On the day of their arrival, Herr Ritter met the Muellers' train at a station a few miles from Melník and then took them north, with a stopover that first night at his home. It was bitterly cold, but not nearly as cold as it would have been at the Polish farm five hundred kilometers to their north. The Ritters were gracious hosts, and the Muellers, who had yet to see their new farm, already felt their situation improving, and for the first time in months they slept well.

They arose early the next day and ate a good breakfast, peppering Ritter with dozens of questions about the farm. As he answered their questions, the Muellers grew even more anxious to see it. It sounded too good to be true, but even if it fell short of his description, it would be better than anything they'd had since Tariverde.

"Are you ready?"

Ritter had crowded them into a buggy as soon as they finished breakfast.

"Yes, we are."

They made their way to Strednitz, a small village with a few German families only fifteen kilometers north of the larger town of Melník. The village was small and dominated by their new home, whose address was of course #1 Strednitz. When she saw it, Johanna gasped, "Ach du meine Güte!"

Herman beamed. "It is truly something."

He looked through the heavy iron gates at the estate. The land in the region was hilly compared to that of Poland, and the house sat at the top of a tall hill. The property was broad, with houses on either side of the main residence and several farm buildings alongside and behind the homes. It would take them time to explore the farm, but first would come the tour of their new home and then the meeting with the three families.

Ritter pulled the buggy to a stop and asked, "Shall we go inside?"

"Lead the way."

Between them and the front porch were more than three dozen steps separated by landings. It had snowed overnight, and someone had swept those steps for them. They made their way up until they reached the front porch, where Johanna turned around to take in the view of the valley.

Ritter said, "It's a lovely view."

"Yes, it is." Then, eyeing the many steps they'd just climbed, she said, "But a person must put forth some effort to enjoy it."

Ritter laughed. "Indeed."

They walked to the entrance, which sat on the right side of the porch. When they made it inside, they felt the warmth of a fire someone had started in order to make their first morning in Strednitz as pleasant as possible. It was a nice welcome. They entered a large entry hall that had a desk in one corner.

"And this hallway can serve as your new office, Herman."

He studied the room carefully. The desk and chair were in good shape, and he was amazed to think that they were there for his use. He didn't know exactly how he'd use them at that point, but he was sure he'd find a purpose.

To the left of the office area was a long, narrow room. It was unfurnished except for hooks on the walls for hanging clothing. Ritter explained that this was a place for the men and children to enter the house with their dirty shoes and clothing. On that day it held the Muellers' belongings that they'd shipped earlier.

Ritter said, "We put your things in here. My wife thought you'd know where they should go."

Johanna said, "I'll take care of them. Thank you so much for getting them this far."

"More than happy to do it. Let's look at the rest of the house, shall we?"

Beyond the mudroom was a winding staircase made of the same beautiful dark wood they would find throughout the house. As they passed the stairs, they beheld something that seemed as if from a dream—a bathroom! While they might have expected it in a house of this quality, it still came as a bit of a surprise, and a pleasant one at that.

They walked into the kitchen and found it to be large and well equipped. Frau Huber had left most of her things, having no way of taking them with her. The pots and pans and utensils in the kitchen, the furniture in the rest of the house, and the carpets and drapery left behind by Frau Huber were things the Muellers couldn't have afforded. Chances were they could have never found such nice things during wartime anyway.

Behind the kitchen was a pantry that was almost as large as the kitchen itself. When Johanna opened the door to it, she was stunned to see an abundance of food on its shelves. There was oil and sugar for the winter, as well as pickles, sauerkraut, jams, jellies, canned vegetables, lard, flour, and everything else a family could need, with plenty left over to meet the needs of others. She learned there were more beets, potatoes, and turnips being stored in the cool cellar, and there was meat in the smokehouse. There was no store in Strednitz, but for the Muellers and the other families living on the farm, one would seldom be needed.

On the rest of the main floor, the part behind the office, there were two large rooms. One was a sitting room lined with large windows that ran from ceiling to floor and opened on a beautiful view. The other was a large interior dining room furnished with a grand old table and a dozen matching chairs. On one wall there was a door that connected to the kitchen. Over the table, hanging from the nine-foot ceiling, was an ornate oval chandelier. The room bespoke an elegance that predated the Hubers.

The children enjoyed the sitting and dining rooms, but they were more interested in seeing the bedrooms upstairs, so they sprang up the steps to check them out, with Rolf leading the way. Herr Ritter came last as Herman and Johanna followed their children. When they reached the second floor, they found a bedroom for each boy, and one for Annelise, in addition to a large one for the parents. And then, wonder of wonders—a second bath.

Johanna was overwhelmed by it all. On the one hand, she was happy to find the bedrooms already furnished, but of all the rooms, the bedrooms seemed the most personal to her, and she could almost feel the presence of the people who'd lived there before, including the Czech family who'd lived there prior to the Hubers. It was disconcerting in a way, but the excited chatter of her children prevented her from dwelling on it.

Herman looked at their friend and said, "Again, how can we ever thank you for all you've done for us?"

"It's my pleasure, Herman. The Hubers were nice people and this place needed another nice German family to live here, and who better than you?"

"When will we meet the others?"

"I think after lunch. It's been a long time since breakfast. We've brought sausages and bread and cheese with us, and it looks like the pantry will provide us with anything else we should need. Let's go eat, then we'll meet the rest."

8

Meeting the Families

Later that morning

"So tell us about the families who share the farm."

Ritter finished his last bite and felt the eyes of the whole Mueller family on him. He wiped his face before answering. "They seem to be nice people, and Frau Huber spoke well of them, especially the Nováks, who I'll introduce first. They can take it from there and introduce the rest, then I'll need to start the trip home if I want to make it to Melník before dark."

Johanna agreed, "Oh, yes! You'll need to get going. There are so few hours of daylight, and I don't like the idea of your traveling alone at night."

"I'll be okay."

"Still, we won't keep you long." Her mind returned to the families. "And you said we'll meet the Nováks before the others?"

"Yes. Filip and Katerina Novák should be first. They've been here the longest, and they can help you to communicate with the rest."

"So, they must speak a little German?"

"Yes, they do. More than a little. They came here from an area where German was commonly spoken, and so German is a second language for them. It isn't perfect for either of them, but very serviceable. The other families know almost no German, or at least they act as if they don't, so when something needs to be said, an order given, or a question answered, it's Filip with the men, and Katerina with the women who'll act as your go-betweens. It's not the best arrangement, perhaps, but you're lucky to have such good people, such good workers, to be top assistants. It would be difficult to manage this farm without them." He stopped talking for a moment before continuing, "They should be coming in a few minutes."

And just then, the Nováks were heard knocking at the door. Johanna wanted to be the one to greet them, but she knew protocol would be for Ritter to do it. After all, he was the one they knew.

The Nováks were ushered into the office, where the Muellers awaited. They lined up facing the Muellers, and their eyes searched for places to look other than directly at the new German family. Neither of the Nováks were tall, and even with heavy winter coats concealing much of their appearance, it was apparent that the wife tended toward plump while Mr. Novák was thin. Still, there was something about him indicating that under that coat was a man of some strength. His hands, disproportionately large and calloused, confirmed the impression, and his face showed the rigors of life as a farmhand. Katerina's hair was straight and long with a touch of gray. She and her husband seemed to be in their fifties.

Standing with them were their three daughters. When Ritter introduced Zuzana, who looked to be around twenty, and her two younger sisters, who were in their teens, he told the Muellers that all the girls still lived at home. Perhaps with daughters so young, the Nováks were only in their forties after all, and it was the hard life of farming that had aged them.

When Ritter finished the introductions, Herman stepped forward to shake Filip's hand and tell him he had a lovely family. The compliment brought a smile to Filip's face, and he returned it. The women weren't sure what to do, so they waited while the men talked for a bit. When the men ran out of the few things they had to say, Ritter announced that it was time for him to leave. He found his coat, and the Muellers walked him to the door, thanking him again for all he'd done for them.

As he started to exit, he turned and said that he had arranged for a local family, also German, to come calling the next day. "The Pöhlmanns are good people, and they'll answer any questions you might have. They have children too, and they can tell you more about schools for German children."

"What time might we expect them?"

"I've told them to come in the mid-afternoon, if that's acceptable."

Johanna said, "It is. And thank you again for thinking of everything we need."

He said his farewells, offered best wishes to all, and was soon on his way to Melník. They watched Ritter leave, and the reality of their situation took hold. While he'd been there, showing them around and handling introductions, it was almost as if he were the owner showing them the place. With him gone, they became more aware that this was theirs now, to live in and to manage. He'd given them the gift of this wonderful farm, but with it would come some challenges. They were now the primary family of an estate with three other families living there, and those families might not care all that much for another German family taking over.

The silence after he left was awkward, and it appeared that the Nováks were waiting on Herman to make the next move.

"So, shall we meet the others?"

"Yes. They're quite anxious to meet the new family. I'll send the girls for them."

Filip gave the word, and the girls left to fetch the other two families. Again there was an awkward silence, but luckily it wasn't long until they heard a knock at the door.

Johanna exclaimed, "Oh my goodness! They don't need to knock again. Herman, go let them in." Herman went to the door, and the two new families crowded into the small office area. Johanna suggested they go to the larger sitting room, and the Nováks led the way with the rest following.

When they'd gathered in the sitting room, she had the Nováks stand next to them. She hoped it would be a way to reassure the others that the old arrangement—with Filip and Katerina acting as assistants and intermediaries—was still in effect.

"Herr and Frau Mueller, allow me to introduce to you the other families on our farm. First, to your left are Jan and Teresa Dvořák, their daughter, and their son."

The families nodded a greeting, then Herman stepped forward to shake Jan's hand. He said something to the man, and he could see that even though Jan nodded his head and pretended to understand, he didn't.

"Filip, tell them we are happy to meet them."

He did, and it brought a smile to their faces. They said something, and Herman knew without translation that it was a thank you. The girl and her younger brother appeared to be around the ages of Rolf and Georg, which suggested the Dvořáks were around the age of the Muellers.

Georg was excited to see a boy his age and said something to him. The boy looked to his parents to see if they knew what had been said, but they didn't appear to understand.

Johanna said, "Georg, they speak a different language than we do."

"Maybe I can learn it."

"I am sure you can, and you can teach them German."

Herman looked at Filip, indicating he'd like to meet the other couple.

"Allow me to introduce the Czernýs, Marek and Veronica, and of course their new baby, little Anna."

The younger couple, hearing their names, nodded a greeting just as the Nováks had done a moment before.

Marek Czerný was a tall, handsome young man, broad-shouldered and showing less deference than the others. He stepped forward to shake hands with Herman, earning him a look of disapproval from the other Czech men.

Johanna asked about the baby, and Filip relayed her question to Veronica. Veronica prattled on for a few minutes, then noticed her husband frowning at her and stopped. Filip translated what she'd said, and Johanna, after hearing it, asked him to tell the Czernýs what a beautiful baby they had, and how little Anna looked like her mother. When Filip had finished, the young couple smiled appreciatively.

Silence followed. Johanna wished she had something prepared she could share with her guests, something sweet to serve with a beverage. She could tell there was a long way to go to establish a relationship, let alone friendship, and she regretted that she hadn't had time to fix something that might start them down that path. The language barrier added to the silence, and it was uncomfortable. Filip and Katerina sensed the awkwardness, so Katerina suggested to her husband that Herman might enjoy a tour of the farm before dark.

Filip asked Herman if he'd like a tour. Herman nodded his enthusiastic approval and suggested the other men join them. Rolf and Georg convinced their father that they should see the farm too, with the Dvořák boy also joining them. Before long the men were leaving, with the women staying behind to help Johanna put things away.

❦ 9 ❦

The First Night in Strednitz

Later that night

She sought his hand under the covers and put hers on top of it. He turned on his side facing her, then took her hand in his. She asked him, "So what do you think of our new home?"

He took a breath, then followed with a slow exhale, the way he did when he wanted to be thoughtful with an answer. "I'll tell you what I think, and when I'm finished, I'll ask you what you think. How's that?"

"That's fair."

"I'll say this about the farm: it's large and it takes time to walk it in the snow. There's a building for every purpose. The property is hilly, as you saw when we arrived, but they tell me the soil is good." He took in another breath. "It was beautiful today, even in snow, and I can't wait to see it in springtime."

"So Filip was a good guide, I take it?"

"Of course. The best. We stopped several times, and when we'd stop he would tell us something about each spot, and at times his words sounded as if he were a young man speaking of a girl he fancied. Even when he spoke of ordinary matters such as what to plant and when to plant it, you could hear the love in his voice."

Johanna said, "Maybe it's because he spoke German, but I liked Filip best of the men on the farm."

"Undoubtedly his speaking German helps, but you have good reason to like him. Filip Novák shows you exactly who he is the moment you meet him, and when I met him today and spent a couple of hours walking the farm with him, I saw an honest man who will be a good worker, a person who can and should be relied upon."

"Should?"

"Yes."

Herman was quiet for a bit, then added, "And if I were not around, he'd be the man I'd want to run the farm in my place."

That puzzled Johanna. "Why would you not be around?"

"There's no guarantee that I'll always be here."

"And where will you go?"

"I have no plans."

She squeezed his hand. "Good, because I would miss this."

"And I as well." He pulled her closer. "Now it's your turn. This house—what do you think of it?"

"It's big and it doesn't seem like something that should belong to us."

"And yet, here we are."

"I know, Herman. But after everything that's happened, I feel I might wake up and find I've been dreaming."

"It was time for luck to come our way."

"It's hard for me to think of us as lucky people."

Herman changed the subject. "You've asked me about Novák. Let me ask you, how was your time with Mrs. Novák?"

"It's Nováková. Did you know that?"

"No."

"It's how they do the names of married women here, and I learned that Mrs. Czerný is called Czerna."

"Okay, I'll do my best to remember that. Anyway, how was it with her?"

"I think she's a good match for her husband, because she also seems to have a good spirit and a trustworthiness about her. I can tell she'll be a great help to me, and I would like to think, even a friend someday.

"I think she was surprised when I told her the story of how we came to be here. She may have made some assumptions about us, but after hearing how our journey hasn't been easy—that we came from Romania and not from Germany—well, to be honest I think it helped close a gap between us."

"That could be," Herman agreed.

"I would imagine the people here in Czechoslovakia don't like Germans much. They won't dare say it aloud, but I'm sure they don't. How could they? When I told her we were from Dobrogea, not Germany, and we had been ordered to leave our home against our wishes, spent two years in Löhr, and were sent to Poland, it set us apart from the Nazis, I think."

"That would be good, but I doubt they'll ever be our friends."

"I suppose not. Although I think she had grown fond of Frau Huber even in the short time she was here."

"Why do you think that?"

"Just the way she spoke of her. She mentioned the different ways that Frau Huber showed kindness to the families."

"And knowing you, you made a note of each of those ways."

"Yes, and I intend to do at least as much."

"My Johanna, I wouldn't expect any different of you."

"She also showed me the cellar. I'll have to show you tomorrow. It's as full of food as the pantry—full of beets, turnips, and potatoes—more than enough food for our family. She told me the winters get so long that the tenant houses run short of what they need, and that Frau Huber made sure to share from the provisions in the big house."

"Good, and it's only right we do the same. They will help us with this big farm, and they should share in what we produce."

"I told her as much, and she seemed thankful. It made me sad to see her so grateful. It was a simple gesture of kindness, an action people should be expected to do for each other."

"It's wartime, dear. Rules change. Things are different. Acts of kindness are rare."

She sighed. "Maybe they shouldn't be."

"Well of course, you're right, but I'm sure other Germans aren't so thoughtful as you."

"Germans. Is that really what we are? I don't think of us that way."

"We may not, but others will see it differently. I suspect many of the people here will think of us as another German family."

"I will always think of myself as a a Tariverdian before I consider myself German."

"We'll never go back there, Johanna. Maybe we're people without a country. Maybe all we have is each other and this wonderful farm, and we should just be content with that."

She was quiet for a moment, then remembered something she'd learned from Katerina. "Did you hear about the summer helpers?"

"Yes, Filip told me about them when he took me past their summer residence."

"Katerina told me there could be as many as ten of them."

"I imagine so. There were that many cots in their dormitory at least."

She chuckled. "It should be interesting when they're all here."

"Yes, that at least."

"Ten more workers—and added to the rest of the people here. This has all been a lot to take in. I'm glad that Katerina has done this before and can help me learn."

"Good, and Mrs. Dvorák . . ."

"Dvoráková," corrected Johanna.

"Okay then, Dvoráková. She seemed nice. Did she stay and help you as well?"

"She did. She was quiet though and hard to read."

"As was her husband, but as you noticed, their German is . . . how shall I say it—limited."

"I'm sure that was the reason. And the other one, the young Veronica, she helped some, but then left when her baby became fussy."

"Our boys seemed quite impressed with young Marek, her husband. They followed him around and laughed at his antics. I don't think Filip cares much for him though."

"Marek looks to be but a boy himself."

"True." His tone changed a bit as he talked. "It's something when you think about it. We have this farm now, and there are three other families who'll depend on our success, and then there will be all those summer workers—girls if I heard correctly—to be fed and looked after."

She said, "Perhaps those girls will be good help."

"True, but for every helping hand comes another mouth to feed."

"Or you could say with every mouth comes two hands. That's a better way to think of it."

Herman said, "We'll figure it out."

"And no one would do it better than you."

He put his lips against her ear and said, "It has been quite a day, but I'm not tired."

She playfully nudged him in the ribs. "You should be, and you need your sleep. You have a farm to show me tomorrow. We don't have to make up for all those nights we spent in the crowded convent and in the small house in Poland on this one night. You've had a nice start. There'll be other nights."

"I'll remember that."

"I have no doubt!"

She couldn't see his smile in their darkened bedroom, but she knew it was there.

10

The Farm

The next morning

It snowed overnight, another snow in a winter when days without snowfall seemed rare. As soon as they finished breakfast, the family bundled for a cold, snowy tour of the farm.

Rolf and Georg begged Herman to let them serve as tour guides for Johanna and Annelise, and he agreed. They began by carefully descending the steps to the bottom of the hill. The snow had covered the steps, canceling the work of the day before. To their left they passed the two-story home of the Nováks, and beyond that, a large building that stored the grain. Next came a barn for hay and straw, a henhouse, and sheds for the various pieces of farm machinery and one for firewood. Beyond all those and stretching out in front of them were the fields where the grains and vegetables would be raised when spring came. The fields were covered in snow, but Herman painted a picture of how green and productive everything would soon become.

Circling behind the house, they made their way up a slight rise to the right, where they found stalls for the pigs, horses, and cows. When they came to one stall, the most impressive animal on the farm stared menacingly back at them.

Annelise wanted to know, "Why is this one not with the others?"

Rolf answered, "He's the bull."

Herman explained that the farm had one of very few breeding bulls in the area, and the animal tended to be somewhat cantankerous, so it was best he be left alone.

Johanna didn't like the looks of the animal and wanted to know why their farm had to be the one to keep him.

"There wouldn't be any calves without him."

She gave him a look of mild disgust.

"And he'll make us money when the neighbors bring cows to be serviced."

"Just send the boys to the house or have them do some errand when that happens. Find an excuse."

"I think, knowing how boys are, sending them away will only make things more interesting."

"Please."

"Sure. For you, anything."

The children noticed their behavior, and it was Rolf who spoke up. "Why are you whispering?"

"Just sharing a secret."

"You've told us not to do that."

"It's okay for the adults."

Rolf wasn't satisfied, but Herman said it was time to move on to the house where the girls would stay.

Annelise's interest picked up. "Girls?"

"Yes, we'll have as many as ten girls from the area living here in summer. There's no possible way we can handle all the planting, weeding, and harvesting without them."

Rolf grinned. "Ten girls, Annelise. Won't that be nice?"

She thought it over and had a question. "Why only girls?"

Herman joked, "Because you are too pretty to have boys around."

She smiled and asked again, "So why is it only girls?"

"According to Filip, there are more girls than boys who want the work, and he's found them to be better workers. With them all staying in the dormitory, it has to be all girls then. We couldn't have boys there too."

They kept moving. At the right of the big house were two more houses, each of them smaller than the Novák family's home. The one farthest from the main house belonged to the Czernýs and the one nearer to the Dvoráks. The Czernýs' home was more of a cottage than a home. As they passed it, young Veronica stepped out and waved, with little Anna bundled against her. Annelise asked her mother if she could go visit and help with the baby. Johanna agreed, although she wasn't sure how her daughter would manage to communicate with the young mother.

Annelise walked up to Veronica and made a gesture indicating she'd love to hold the baby, and Veronica nodded yes, then motioned for her to come inside. It would be an hour before Annelise returned to the main house. When she did, Annelise told her mother about her visit. Not only did she get to hold the baby, but she was allowed to feed the infant some cereal mixed with milk.

Later that afternoon, a couple pulled through the gates of the property and made their way up the steps to the door, and there was a young girl with them. When their knock was heard, Georg raced to the door, with his mother close behind, chiding him to let her answer it. Georg obediently stepped behind his mother and peeked around her as she opened the door.

The couple at the door greeted Johanna in German, introducing themselves as Günter and Olexa Pöhlmann and their daughter Minna. Johanna invited them in and shut the door behind them. She told them her name, and Georg stepped from behind his mother and also told them his name. Johanna was irritated, but the Pöhlmanns thought it was cute. She invited them into the sitting room and sent Georg to find Rolf, Annelise, and their father.

As they waited for the rest of the family to come, they engaged in some small talk about the weather. Soon Herman and the children arrived, and Johanna handled the introductions. Everyone took a seat, and Herman asked the Pöhlmanns to share their story. Günter told them that they'd lived in a German enclave like Tariverde and were relocated to Strednitz at nearly the same time the Muellers were being sent to Löhr. They'd been assigned to a farm down the road, one not nearly as big as this property, but just right for them. Olexa added that soon after they were moved in, they met the Hubers and became good friends with them. She said they were lovely people, especially Frau Huber. Günter had tried to help with the farm after Herr Huber's passing, but it was too much.

Günter Pöhlmann then asked Herman and Johanna to tell them about their family. Herman deferred to Johanna, knowing she'd do the story more justice than he, and he was right. As she talked, the Pöhlmanns listened with interest, interrupting only a few times with questions or memories her story had raised. Of course there were sad moments in those memories, but on that first meeting it was better to remember happier times. The more they shared, the more they felt like old friends. For the Muellers it was great to have another family nearby with whom they shared so much. For the Pöhlmanns, it would be wonderful to have friends again in the Hubers' home.

During the exchange, Johanna had sent the children to the kitchen for a tray of pastries that she'd prepared after the morning's tour. She'd selected some of the best apples from the cellar and baked a strudel using a recipe she'd learned from her mother. With coffee being in short supply, she'd brewed an ersatz blend of ingredients given to her by Katerina Novák. Soon the Mueller children came in with trays of food and beverages. The adults were served, then the children. Since it was a special occasion, the children got a small cup of the hot beverage to go with their strudel, but theirs was highly diluted with milk. Still, they felt very grown up.

Herman thought it time to address the main reason for their gathering. "So Herr Ritter has told me you know about the schooling for our children. We're anxious to get them started. What can you tell us?"

Pöhlmann set his coffee cup down. "Before I answer that, allow me to say that the strudel was delicious."

Johanna smiled at the compliment, "I'm glad you enjoyed it. But please, I want to hear your answer to my husband's question."

Günter continued, "Rolf here will go to a school in the village of Vysoka. It's only a short kilometer from here, and he'll have no problem getting to and from it each day." Then he looked at Annelise. "You are nearly the age of our Minna. There's no school for you nearby. It's necessary for you to board and attend school in Prague." Looking at Rolf, he said, "You will go to the school in Vysoka for one more year after this one, then you'll join your sister in Prague." He turned to look at Georg, who was waiting to hear his situation. "And the little fellow will begin attending school with his brother next fall, then he'll be on his own the following year."

Annelise was unhappy to hear this. She'd already had enough of boarding during her time in Warthbrücken, but at least there, Rolf was with her. Soon, she'd be going off to a strange school in a new city with only Minna, whom she'd just met. It didn't help that their new house seemed so nice, and soon she'd be leaving it for several months.

She tried not to show her distress, but Olexa Pöhlmann couldn't avoid noticing. "It will be okay, Annelise. Our Minna will be with you, and there's room for you to live in the house where she boards, so you'll have a friend when you start, and soon many more, just like our Minna. It's a lovely school with good teachers, and you'll learn there. There's no one here to teach you."

Annelise took some comfort in that, and she knew there was no alternative. Perhaps with circumstances such as these a different mother might have allowed her daughter to be done with her education, but Johanna had been deprived of a formal education in her little village, and she would have none of that for Annelise.

Annelise looked at the other girl, then back at the Pöhlmanns. "How often does Minna get to come home?"

Herr Pöhlmann took the question. "It's forty-five kilometers to Prague from here, and we don't like her traveling by herself, so it's not as often as any of us would like."

"When will I start?"

"We've brought Minna home so she could meet you and help you get settled in Prague. We're taking her back the day after tomorrow, and it would be a good time for you to come with us and get started."

Johanna said, "I want to see where she lives and where she'll go to school. I hope it will suit you for me to come along."

"Of course, we would be happy for any or all of you to come."

Johanna looked to Herman, who said, "It will just be her mother for now. The boys and I will join Johanna the next time she goes to Prague, and when we do, the whole family can have a few days in the city. A little holiday if you will."

"Then it's set. We'll leave early the morning after tomorrow, make the trip to Prague, get the girls settled, then return the following day."

"Very good."

They talked for a few more minutes, then as the conversation started to lag, the Pöhlmanns sensed it was time to go.

Olexa said, "Please allow Minna and me to help with the dishes and trays."

"Oh no, the children can help me."

"Well, it was delicious, Johanna, and the company was wonderful."

As they all stood at the door saying their goodbyes, Herman said, "When you return from Prague, the boys and I will have dinner for you as our way of thanking you for getting Annelise settled."

Johanna was a bit shocked at that. Never had Herman Mueller cooked a meal. He looked at her and, with the slightest grin, said, "I'm sure Mrs. Novák will be more than happy to help with the preparations."

Johanna tried not to smile but couldn't help herself. "I'm sure she will."

The Pöhlmanns thought it sounded like a perfect plan and turned to leave, but before they'd taken two steps, Minna turned around and came to Annelise. She put her arms around her and whispered, "It will be all right. I'll be there to make sure."

Annelise, tears welling up at Minna's kindness and at the prospect of what lay ahead, whispered a thank-you in return.

When they'd taken their leave, Johanna said, "What nice people, and what a lovely thing for Minna to say to you, Annelise."

Annelise forced a smile. "She's nice, and I'm sure she'll be a good friend and help me find my way, but I'd give anything if Rolf were coming too."

Rolf nodded, an indication he'd prefer that as well.

Georg said, "But at least you get to go. And Rolf gets to go to school. I must wait." He stamped his foot. "I don't like being the one who gets left out."

Johanna mussed his hair. "It will pass all too quickly, my little man."

⤲ **11** ⤳

Winter Meeting

Late February 1942

Filip Novák and Herman sat in the office talking about the summer to come. Outside, yet another big snow was falling that afternoon, and it seemed as if spring might never make its way to Strednitz. The men knew it would, and that if they weren't prepared for it and the summer that followed, they'd fall behind, and the next winter would be difficult. It was a good farm, but in order to provide for all the families, with some left over for the summer girls and more still to help feed the people in the cities and the troops on the front lines, careful planning would be required.

"So here is a plan I put in place with Herr Huber." Filip had a hand-drawn map of the place. It was a bit crude, but a good representation of the property. Each field was labeled with a different set of Roman numerals, and each numeral stood for a different usage, with root crops and grains in rotation with grasses and clovers. Under the Roman numerals Filip had indicted what specific types of crops in each category would be planted by year. It was very intricate, but Herman understood the beauty of it, as it took into consideration the health of the soil over the years. Filip explained, "Last year was the second year of my three-year cycle of crops, so that means we're moving to year three. In each field the III designates next year's plantings."

Filip allowed him some time, then asked, "Do you approve, Herr Mueller?"

"You've lived here for more than a decade, Filip. How could I question what you know of this place? So of course, let's go to year three of your plan."

Filip had a shy grin. "In fact, we'd already begun it when we planted the winter wheat last fall."

Herman smiled. "Of course you did; it was a wise decision."

"That is very kind of you, but to repeat myself, you're the head of the farm now, and if you think things should be done another way, then that is what we'll do."

Herman leaned back in his chair and looked at Filip. "I may be head of this farm, but you are the one who knows it, and I will always pay close attention to what you suggest."

"Thank you."

"So Filip, tell me more about the summer girls."

"I have some news on that. We've spoken with the girls from last summer, and a few of them will be returning. Katka and I have asked those who plan to return to help recruit girls who want work, and we have spoken with some families in the area ourselves." He stopped suddenly and looked at Herman. "I hope that is suitable."

"Of course it is. You are in a much better position to recruit the summer help. For one thing, people in the area know you, and for another you speak their language. It only makes sense that we trust you on this."

"We won't disappoint you."

Herman looked at the man with respect for what he knew and with appreciation for how good he was with the other men. "There's no need to speak of disappointing us. I doubt you would ever let us down, because to let us down would be to let the farm down. I know above all else, you want what is best for this place, and that's what I want as well."

If Filip resented a second German family taking over the farm, he never showed it. He was a practical man who understood the situation he was in, but more than that, he understood that the well-being of everyone on the farm depended on cooperation. Herman, too, was a practical man whose focus was always on what needed to be done. He never carried himself in a way that indicated superiority. He'd show himself to be willing to pitch in and work alongside the others, becoming one of them as he did. Herman and Filip were forging a good partnership, one that Herman hoped would carry over to Jan and Marek.

✤ **12** ✤

First Spring

1942

Just as Johanna had told Georg they would, the days passed quickly. The snow started to melt, and the green shoots of the wheat, rye, and rapeseed plants started to show. Before long, it would be time to plant oats and barley, and then the root crops would follow.

As the days grew longer, there were babies being born all over the farm. First came the calves, products of the work of the bull, then the lambs and piglets. Some of the hens were put in a separate pen with a rooster, and before long they were sitting on nests full of eggs that would provide the next generation of hens for laying and for eating. While all of this was happening, the sheep had to be sheared and the wool made ready for spinning.

The days were long and filled with planting, cultivating, and harvesting. In what little spare time the families had, they worked in their own gardens. When summer came, they'd enjoy what they grew, while putting away as much as they could in their pantries and cellars. Another long and potentially difficult winter loomed.

With Rolf in school most days, Georg followed his father and the other men around the farm, helping when he could, asking dozens of questions, and getting in the way more often than not. As the days lengthened, his hair began to turn blond and his skin brown. Soon his shirt would be discarded and his summer shorts donned. Once again, he was shoeless, except when conditions required shoes.

He loved following the men and having fun with the Dvoráks' little son. They somehow learned to communicate, their language a combination of German, Czech, and signs. In spite of this burgeoning friendship, the days when Rolf was home from school were the best days for Georg. He adored his brother, and he liked having him to share his chores and adventures.

On one such day, as Rolf and Georg stepped inside the henhouse to gather eggs, they immediately knew something was amiss. The hens were unsettled. The boys looked around and discovered the reason for all the commotion. There was a porcupine in the henhouse. How he'd made it inside was a mystery, but animals are ingenious when it comes to food. It didn't appear that he'd harmed the hens, and there were no eggshells around. Maybe some grain scattered on the floor had attracted his attention, but whatever the cause, this young porcupine had found a way inside and could find no way out. It was up to the boys to make that happen.

The hens scurried out the open door into the pen, glad to be away from the frightened animal who cowered in a dark corner. The boys stepped outside and shut the door so they could discuss what they should do next. Of course, the obvious answer would have been to find one of the men and have him deal with the creature, but Rolf wanted to show their father how grown-up he was and how he was able to take care of situations like this himself. Georg, always in awe of his brother, was not about to defy him.

"I think we should drown him in the pond."

Georg wasn't sure that was the best idea. "How can we do that without getting quills in us? I hear they hurt and they're hard to get out."

"We'll have to be careful. I think we need a wooden box or something similar that will hold him so his quills don't get us."

Georg wasn't sure what they were going to do with that box, but Rolf had a plan, and that was good enough. He remembered seeing a small wooden keg near the animal pens, and Rolf thought that could work. They'd just need some sort of lid. They looked around and found a piece of wood that was large enough to cover the keg's opening. So with the materials obtained, the plan was set in motion. Rolf would sneak up on the porcupine and trap it under the keg, then Georg would slide the board underneath it. They'd combine their efforts, Georg holding the lid while Rolf carefully turned the keg over, then they'd carry it to the pond and throw it as far as they could and watch the porcupine drown.

They made their way back into the henhouse with the keg and the board in hand. Rolf crept up on the agitated porcupine with the keg as a shield, its open end toward the creature. The animal bristled, but somehow Rolf was able to move quickly enough to trap it without doing harm to himself. He held down on the keg, keeping the animal from escaping even though it was frantically trying to free itself and showing surprising strength as it did.

Rolf tipped one side of the keg ever so slightly, and Georg began sliding the board under the opening he created. It became more difficult as the board reached the porcupine, but with Rolf's encouragement Georg finally succeeded in getting it underneath. Step one of the plan was a success.

"Now this is the hard part. You have to put your hands under each end of the board and make sure it's tight against the keg as I turn it over, otherwise he'll escape and we'll both get hurt."

Georg did exactly as he was told, and somehow the two boys managed to get the keg inverted with the lid on top. The porcupine had slid to the other end, and it was clawing at the wood trying to get out. It was easy to tell its mood hadn't improved, and any mistake at this point would cause them misery. Rolf had his right hand under the keg and his left hand on top while Georg walked alongside. They slowly made their way across the lot and then down the slight slope to the deeper end of the pond. When they reached a point that Rolf thought would work, he deftly threw the keg, lid, and porcupine into the pond. Not surprisingly, the keg and lid floated, and for a moment there was no activity from the animal. Within seconds he surfaced. The boys watched him battle the water for a bit, then swim effortlessly as if he'd been a beaver in another life. As he neared the shore, the boys took off running, with Rolf speeding away from his younger brother.

Georg was sure the porcupine would come after them to exact his revenge, and he'd be the first one the animal would reach. He needn't have worried; the porcupine had no interest in the boys, seeking instead the weeds and cover. For years after that, Rolf and Georg shared a private joke about the fact that porcupines can swim, but that night at the dinner table when they told their parents, it wasn't quite as funny. Johanna was appalled, and Herman laid into the boys, letting them know they were lucky not to have been turned into pincushions by the animal. When he asked them why they didn't just leave the door to the house open and let the poor thing escape, Rolf said, "I thought he might eat the chickens."

Herman said, "Boys! Porcupines don't eat chickens. He was there for the grain. You put yourselves at risk for no reason. Come get one of us next time."

Rolf lowered his head, and tears streamed down Georg's cheeks.

Rolf, unhappy to see Georg upset, told their parents that it was his decision to drown the animal and that Georg shouldn't get in trouble. While Herman and Johanna were moved by that, they didn't want to let him off completely. They told Rolf not to do that again, and he assured them he wouldn't. Georg, seeing his brother accept the blame and happy they weren't in much trouble, wiped the tears off his cheeks and smiled at his brother. Dinner resumed, and the boys made sure the talk moved to other topics.

In a few more weeks, Annelise would come home from school, the summer help would arrive, and the first summer on the farm would begin.

The Nováks had contacted three girls who planned to return. These three came out to the farm a few weeks early so that they could meet the Muellers and prepare their dormitory for summer occupation. After a long winter of sitting idle, the building needed to be swept and aired out, and bedding placed on each of the eight cots that would be used that summer.

It would have been better if there had been ten girls, because the work in the fields would progress more quickly, but in the end the Nováks could only find eight girls to help out. While eight could get a lot done each day—whether it be bundling the wheat and stacking it, cultivating the soil around the beets, or gathering them up when the plow turned them over—eight girls weren't ten. Each girl would have to make five trips down the rows, where it would have been only four with a full crew. Machines would have helped with the work, and in fact there was a morning in late spring a new tractor was delivered to the farm. Herr Huber had ordered it before his death. Fuel was in short supply during wartime, so the men moved it to a shed where it sat idle for the remainder of the war. So with no machinery, a diminished summer crew spent long days filled with unrelenting labor in the fields at Strednitz.

Sometimes the boys and Annelise helped, with each of them taking a row. Georg would help one of the summer girls with her rows, usually the one who fell behind the others. The girls loved six-year-old Georg and had fun ruffling his hair and teasing him. While Georg understood very little of their teasing, he enjoyed every moment of it. Rolf took it all in while wishing that he was either Georg's age or older than the twelve-year-old he'd soon be. Annelise wanted to befriend the summer help, but her poor Czech and their poor German made it hard to communicate. Still, the youngsters worked alongside the summer girls and helped make up for the shortage.

The women on the farm sometimes helped in the fields too, but most of their time was spent preparing meals for the field crews. Johanna was a good cook, but preparing food for so many people was something new. Fortunately, Katerina had experience and was able to help her manage. The other women were also helpful, but Veronica Czerný was often preoccupied with her little one, and farm life seemed challenging for her. Perhaps she'd come from a family where not much had been expected of the daughters. Still, she was willing to learn. Johanna made sure the young mother had help with her baby as well as with her garden when needed, and she heard Dekuju so many times, she soon understood what it meant.

Baby Anna became more active as the summer went on, crawling and finding mischief to get into, and her mother appeared to be tired most of the time. By the end of the summer, Veronica Czerný was pregnant again but showing little excitement for it. Marek strutted around, bragging to the other men that there was more than one bull on the farm, and Novák let him know he considered that to be inappropriate. Marek flashed anger, then sulked for a few days.

Herman noticed the strained relationship and questioned Novák about it one evening when none of the others were around. When he heard of Marek's bragging, he shook his head and told Novák that young men like to boast. Novák told him that Marek was one to keep an eye on, and Herman gave him a quizzical look but didn't ask him to explain. To him, Marek was strong and a good worker. He had a beautiful young wife and a second child on the way. Herman couldn't imagine there would be any trouble from him.

———

By late summer, the grains had been threshed and stored, and the wheat straw bundled for the animals' stalls. The hay had been gathered and piled up to serve as additional nutrition for the animals in winter. The rapeseed had been turned into cooking oil, the cabbages harvested and canned as kraut.

All the shelves were full again, and the bins in the cellar filled with root crops. Winter could do its worst; the four families at Strednitz were ready.

Excess produce had been sold, and the summer girls paid in part with money, and in part with food for their families. When they left in late summer, the place grew quiet again. It was a relief for the women of the farm, not having those eight additional mouths to feed, but the girls' liveliness added something to the place, and it wasn't the same without them. All the girls promised they'd return in the summer of 1943, but by then things could change.

Soon it was time for the Mueller children to go to school, and this time all three would go. There was some sadness when Annelise went back to Prague with Minna, but less than when she had gone there in January.

Rolf and Georg attended school in Vysoka. Georg's first year there would be the last one for his brother. The school was a small one, and while there were rooms for each grade level of Czech children, there was just one room for the German children and only one teacher assigned for all eight grades.

"Georg, don't do anything to embarrass me. You hear?"

He looked at his brother. It was their first day of school, and they were making their way to Vysoka together.

"Embarrass you?"

"Yes. Just sit there and be quiet. Don't make a spectacle of yourself. All the other kids will know you're my brother, and if you do something stupid, it'll make me look bad."

"I can't talk?"

"Only when the teacher asks you a question or tells you to, and then be quick about it."

Georg stopped his bike and put his feet on the ground. He'd been excited about being in school with his brother. He'd pictured Rolf sitting right next to him, helping him with his lessons, never imagining that Rolf wouldn't be excited to have him there.

"You sound like you don't want me at the school."

"I want you there, I just don't like it that you will be in the same room with me, and I don't want you bringing any attention to yourself. Leave the silly stuff at home."

Georg sniffled. "I don't want to go if that's how it is."

"You must go to school. Now get back on your bike."

The boy reluctantly resumed riding, but his excitement had disappeared. When he got to school that day, he sat quietly and listened, wishing he were home roaming the farm and helping his father. The teacher was a young lady who'd been coaxed into taking the job a day or two before school started, and she might have noticed his unhappiness had she been more experienced or more interested. She hated that first day of school almost as much as Georg, and by the fourth day, she'd be gone and a new young girl would take her place. Four more teachers would be hired before the year was out. It wasn't so much that the students were unruly or difficult to teach. They weren't perfect by any means, but if they acted up and their parents heard about it, there'd be trouble for them at home. So behavior was seldom an issue. It was more that the young teachers were ill-prepared to teach the required subjects to all the grades in the room, and with very few materials available to them, no one to mentor them through the tough times, and very little pay, teaching the German children was incredibly hard.

᭥ 13 ᭥

The Farm in Fall

Autumn 1942

With the children back in school, the farm crew finished the harvest, planted the winter grains, and prepared other fields for spring planting. As winter approached, three hogs were killed and butchered, with the meat taken to the smokehouse for curing. At the beginning of the butchering, Herman let the men know they each family would get a share of the meat for winter. While the men had hoped that would be the case, they were thrilled to hear that Herman and Johanna would do as the Hubers had done before them. When the boys came home from school on the day of the butchering and learned what had happened, Rolf grew quiet while Georg pouted. The reactions weren't so much about those animals as about the piglets the boys had raised and turned into pets during the summer. Rolf and Georg realized that when another fall rolled around, it would be their pigs that were killed. Herman explained to the boys that providing food for families was the role of the pigs; it was what they were brought into the world to do. He reminded them that they enjoyed their mother's Schwein schnitzel, her Braten, and her Kassler. The boys told Herman they would never eat those dishes again. Their resistance lasted less than a week.

A few days later, the Pöhlmanns came to call. By then, work was slowing, and Johanna thought it would be nice to invite them for lunch. Much of the conversation, for the men at least, centered on the growing season they'd just finished and on plans for the season to come. The women talked about the children, and Frau Pöhlmann shared that they'd just received a letter from their oldest, Fritz, a soldier on the Eastern Front. He reported that he was safe and doing well, and he wrote glowingly of the successes of the Germans. What Olexa didn't share was that much of the letter, particularly the parts about the war, sounded little like their son, as if he were choosing his words carefully. She did share that sometimes the intervals between his letters grew long, and while those delays were always due to the logistics of getting mail from the front, she and Günter worried every day until a letter arrived.

The conversation turned to Minna and Annelise. Letters from the girls came more frequently and were full of talk of classmates, teachers, and schoolwork. Occasionally, boys' names would appear in their letters, something that raised concern with their parents even though they knew the girls weren't children anymore.

After lunch was over, the men went to the office while their wives moved from the dining room to the kitchen. As Johanna stacked the dishes on the counter, she turned to Olexa. "Is it as difficult as I imagine it to be?"

Olexa knew Johanna was asking about her Fritz. "Having our son off fighting somewhere in the east, you mean?"

Johanna put down the drying cloth and said, "Yes."

Olexa placed her cup on the table and looked at Johanna. "Every day when I wake up, I think this might be the day we get the letter telling us we've lost him. Every night as I lie in bed I think about him somewhere in Russia, freezing and missing us and scared that he might not live through another day. There's no way to tell you how awful that is."

Johanna could feel every raw emotion of Olexa's words, relating to it as a mother would while thinking about her own boys and hoping they'd never be in the situation poor Fritz was in. Johanna folded the drying cloth and walked to the table to sit by her friend. The rest of the dishes could wait. Her friend needed her. "I think you've said it very well."

———

In the office, Günter was quiet, and Herman knew why that might be. "I'm sure you're worried about Fritz. I know I would be."

Günter sat his cup on the desk, leaned forward, and in a quiet voice said, "May I say something that must remain here in this room?"

"Absolutely, my friend."

"I go crazy with worry some days. When the worry comes on, I just work harder to make it go away, but when it's quiet in the evening, there's no way to avoid thinking about it. There was one day it started to rain and the lightning flashed and soon came the thunder. I jumped even though I knew it was coming. It was like the noise of war—like an exploding shell—and I thought of my Fritz and how he hears such noises every day and dozens of times, and he must worry the next one is for him."

Herman tried to think of something to comfort his friend. "I'm sure he'll be home at the end of all this, and he'll receive all the honors and benefits his service deserves, and all the love he's been missing."

Günter tilted his head to the right a bit, considering Herman's comment. "We can only wait and hope."

————

In the kitchen, Johanna had taken Olexa's hands in hers, offering silent comfort. Olexa broke their silence. "I wish our ancestors had moved to America instead of Romania."

Johanna thought that an odd thing to say. "Yes?"

"My son might be safe now if that had been the case. Instead, our ancestors chose to stay in Europe and within reach of the Nazis."

"America is in the war now, Olexa. Maybe instead of fighting for Germany, Fritz would be an American soldier coming to Europe to fight Germans."

————

In the office, Günter picked up his cup and said, "This honor you just spoke of. Sometimes, I'm not sure there's any honor to this."

Herman started to assure him there would be, but he wasn't so sure himself, so he remained quiet.

"If you think about it, German boys are fighting on the soil of other countries, and what justifies this? How is there honor in this? It would be one thing if Fritz were on German soil fighting to protect German families, but to be part of an invading army, I have some trouble seeing honor there. What cause is it that he and the others are fighting for? And if the horrible rumors about the work camps are true, then to fight for people who do such things would be something other than honorable, I think."

Herman tried to console him. "When soldiers reach the battlefield, their politics are of survival, their philosophies are of getting home to their families, their dreams are of a future with a woman who will bear their children. Causes are for those safe in cities far from the fields of battle. Boys fight just to return home, and they shouldn't be held accountable for the delusions and depravities of the men who send them to war. It's only important that he come home to you. Everything else can be dealt with after that."

Günter, with tears welling, said, "I just want him home."

————

At the table, Olexa patted Johanna's hand. "I worry for your three, if this goes much longer."

"My three? I don't think Annelise would ever be called, and I pray this will be settled before our boys are of age to serve."

Olexa shifted in her chair, unsure if she should make her point more obvious, then proceeded to do so. "Your third is Herman."

"Herman! He'll be forty soon. They won't be coming for a man of his age—a farmer with families to feed, a farmer who provides food for the troops. No, he'll be safe, I'm sure."

"I would hope so, but how long will it be before they run out of young Germans? How many more Ukrainians and Romanians and Bohemians can they convince to fight? Who will they come for next if not the very young? And then it might be older men such as Herman."

Johanna grew pale. "Oh, this horrid war!"

————

Herman asked, "Did you bring your pipe, Günter?"

"I did. And you have tobacco?"

"A little. We don't grow much of it, but it sells well and I keep some for special times."

"Shall we have a smoke as we think of our children and pray the war will be over soon and everyone back where they should be?"

"Let's."

They put the tobacco in their pipes. Herman took a spill to the fireplace and lit the thin strip of wood, then lit their pipes. The men sat quietly and smoked, one worried about his son at war, the other worried the tide of war might be turning despite the "news" of glorious German successes. If the tide was indeed turning, then Herman's time at Strednitz might be but a pleasant interlude followed by an unspeakable nightmare.

⤳ **14** ⤵

First Christmas at Strednitz

1942

Fall left as quickly as it came, and the long, cold winter of central Europe took hold. The bright spot of winter, even in wartime, was Christmas, and that was true at Strednitz. December found Johanna busy with her baking and excited at the thought Annelise would soon be home. Soon, she'd have her whole family together again, if only for a few days.

The smells from her kitchen were almost too much for Rolf and Georg, and they took turns getting in trouble for trying to sneak a baked treat from under their mother's always-watchful eye. Occasionally she'd allow them to have one, especially if a batch of lebkuchen didn't meet her standards. The boys loved her lebkuchen even when a batch was slightly overdone. They could barely finish their treats before she had another batch baking in the oven.

Herman was nearly as bad, and one day as he passed through her kitchen, Johanna caught him trying to sample some cookies as they cooled on the shelf. She playfully slapped his hand as if he were one of the boys, then allowed him to have just one. He smiled at her as he savored the cookie, and for a moment there was only the peacefulness of a kitchen at Christmas.

When Annelise returned from Prague, it became even more like Christmastime. The only thing to dampen their spirits was a letter from Peter telling them that another son had been called into service. Two were serving in the Heer, with one of them on the Eastern Front and another stationed in France. A third son was in Crimea, while their fourth son was still at home, but for how much longer would be anyone's guess. Peter's sons were special to Herman because of the bond he and his older brother had developed in the dark days after their parents died.

When they received Peter's news, the war became even more immediate. More than likely, Georg would never be called to service, but Rolf would soon be twelve, and while he was still young, he was getting ever closer to an age that he could be called. Herman prayed for the safety of his nephews, prayed that neither of his boys would be drafted, then prayed that he would never be called away from his family. Johanna offered the same prayers, adding a fervent wish for peace for young men everywhere no matter which flag they served.

On the afternoon of Christmas Eve, they loaded into their buggy and made the trip to Melník for a party at the Ritters'. It was a festive evening. They knew most of the people there, and they met some new families, broadening their circle of German friends. There was laughter, singing, food, and drink, and the Muellers celebrated late into the night. Their spirits were high as they loaded the buggy for the trip home. The sun had long since set, but the moon was out, lighting their way.

It was a frigid night, and the family huddled together to keep warm. Herman lowered the leather curtain to keep the cold from their faces, and it helped a bit. Still, to see the road, he was forced to lean forward and peer through the curtain's narrow slit. He would have preferred a better view, but the small amount of relief the curtain provided was worth the challenge it created.

Johanna suggested they sing Christmas songs to keep warm, and soon all five of them were joining in. It was so cold that even bundled together with the shield in place, their voices had a tremor, and their teeth chattered all the while. They were nearly frozen when they got home that Christmas Eve, and they would never venture out on such a cold night again, but they were as happy as they'd felt in years and hoped that things would be better in the new year.

It snowed on Christmas morning, and the mood was festive in all the houses on the farm. Johanna had knitted new caps and mittens for the children and spent some of the money earned that year on clothes for school. There was a simple toy for Georg, but not much more than that.

After breakfast that day, Annelise looked through the big windows at the falling snow. There were several hills on the farm, and it occurred to her they'd be perfect for skiing. She mentioned this to her parents, and Johanna thought, *Skis! Something for next Christmas!*

Christmas Day was very different for the young soldiers they knew. Peter Mueller's oldest son was among German soldiers who had been encircled by

Soviet troops outside of Stalingrad. It wasn't certain on this day if they would be relieved by German troops or if they'd be captured or killed by the Red Army. Frostbite worked at his fingers and toes, food was growing short, and his misery could not have been greater. He had his doubts as he sat there, cold and alone, that he'd ever see Christmas with his family again.

One younger brother was on a train headed east. He'd been stationed in occupied France—not the worst assignment of the war—but with the situation deteriorating near Leningrad, he was being reassigned there. His life in the year ahead would bring much greater peril. He hadn't let his parents know of his new assignment, not wanting to ruin their Christmas. As the train passed through Germany not far from his home, he thought of his parents and his younger brother. To be so close to them yet unable to see them was almost worse than being far away.

The third of the four brothers was stationed in the Crimean Peninsula. It had been a difficult year, but ultimately a successful one with the surrender of Soviet forces in the fall of 1942. While he assumed he would remain stationed there to help hold the strategic region for Germany, nothing was for sure.

The youngest of Peter and Britta Mueller's sons was still home with his parents, but he expected to be part of the Luftwaffe before another Christmas came. They treasured their day with him, but knowing he might soon join his brothers in the service, there was a gloomy feel in the home of Peter Mueller.

Young Fritz Pöhlmann was being treated for wounds near a town in Russia whose name would be little noted in the accounts of the war. His wounds were serious, and care was minimal at best, so his outlook was poor. He came in and out of consciousness and called his mother's name.

✎ 15 ✎

A Change Coming

1943

On a night in late February, Johanna found Herman in his office engrossed in the field plan for the coming spring. She came up behind his chair and put her hands on his shoulders. "Are you sure you're okay with this?"

He knew she wasn't referring to the plan nor the touch of her hands on his shoulders. He rubbed his chin, disliking his winter beard and thinking it was about time to shave it, then answered, "I've said I am."

She massaged his shoulders, feeling some tension there. "But sometimes we say what we feel we should say, and not what we really mean. Is this one of those times?"

He turned to face her. "It will be fine. She's your sister and he's your brother-in-law. They're family, and we'll make room for them. He chuckled. "Although our children won't be all that happy having to share bedrooms again."

"Well, it's a good lesson for them. But then, I suppose they have already had more lessons than children should have."

"Other children have had it far worse. We have this big house with plenty of room. I'm only concerned about adding more mouths to feed, that's all it is."

"But Elsa will be a great help, and I'm sure Detlef will do his best to help too."

He reached up and took hold of her hands. "He's been injured, and we've been told he doesn't get around all that well. I think he won't be of much help to us."

"Perhaps he can be your lead assistant—a pair of eyes and ears for you, and a voice with the men when you're not around."

He had the hint of a smile at the corners of his mouth. "I have that already with Filip."

"I know, but more help is always good. Once Detlef learns how things are done here, you'll see, he'll carry more than his share of the load."

His smile grew, but he offered no response, so she continued. "Detlef has had a difficult time. The fall took a lot out of him. No one could have experienced so many injuries and recovered, and from what we hear his care was poor."

He let go of her hands. "Johanna, even before he was hurt, he wasn't very good at anything he did. You know I am fond of your sister Elsa. She's not you, but she has many of your good qualities, and who wouldn't like that? But Detlef, let's be honest, he's not . . ."

"He's not you, Herman. My luck was much better when father found you. The funny thing is, at first, everyone thought Elsa was the lucky one with her match."

"Detlef was a smooth talker, and he always put on a good show. I'm sure your parents were impressed at first."

"Detlef talks big, but you are one who does, and seeks no attention for it." She kissed him on the forehead. "I'm so lucky to have you. And I can't thank you enough for letting Elsa's family come live with us while they look for a new situation."

✆ 16 ✆

The Lehmann Family

Two weeks later

The weather was atrocious on the day that Detlef, Elsa, and Emma Lehmann arrived. It was raining, turning everything into a sea of mud and soaking their few belongings on the wagon. Herman came down the steps and directed Detlef up the road to a higher spot where it would be easier to unload the wagon. He had Rolf unhitch the team and take them to a stall that had been prepared for them. The animals were thin and hungry, but they drank liters of water before turning to their food.

Everyone pitched in and unloaded the wagon, and after several trips they'd moved everything to the mudroom. They dried themselves off then took the parents' things to Georg's room and Emma's belongings to Annelise's room. It was a temporary move for many of Emma's things, because in a few days she would be moving to Prague to attend school with Annelise and Minna.

At dinner that evening, Herman sat quietly while the sisters and Detlef carried on. Georg and Rolf occasionally tried to interject something into the conversation, probably to impress their cousin. Emma paid little attention to any of it. She was a beautiful girl, looking like her mother at that age, but she never smiled, seeming a bit disheartened by everything that had happened, and when there was talk of her new school, it only seemed to make things worse. She'd left all her old friends behind, first in Romania, then the new ones she'd made in Germany. Now she would go to a new school and start over, and what guarantee was there that if she made new friends, her family wouldn't move again? No one would fault her for sitting quietly while the adults chattered and her two cousins acted like goofy young boys.

After dinner, the two brothers-in-law went to Herman's office for a smoke. Detlef was quieter than in the dining room earlier. After a pause, he took his pipe from his mouth. "I know this is an imposition on our part, and I tried to talk Elsa out of asking for your help, but in the end, we knew no other way to go."

"It's okay, Detlef. I understand that your injuries have made it difficult for you to provide for your family."

Detlef was appreciative of the kindness. He suspected Herman was aware things weren't going all that well before his fall, but he hoped his brother-in-law understood that his lack of success wasn't his fault. Detlef felt he was never a good fit for the work they had given him. He should have been assigned to some bureaucratic position—something in an office with a desk, something of importance to the running of the country and the winning of the war. He felt the factory job was beneath his talents.

"I plan to be of help to you. I am healing a little, and although I'll never again be the young man who could do anything he wanted, I promise I'll not be a burden to you."

"I'm sure you'll do your best."

"And we know our wives will do a wonderful job of running the house." He paused, took a draw on his pipe, then continued, "So tell me more about this farm."

In the kitchen, Johanna and Elsa were cleaning up. They'd laughed at old stories and shed a tear or two at what they'd lost. When their work was done, they took a seat at the kitchen table, waiting for the men to finish their after-dinner smoke.

Elsa spoke first. "We can't thank you enough for taking us in. To be honest, without you . . . well, I don't know."

"You were in a difficult spot. With the injuries to Detlef you needed time and a place for him to recover, and I know the situation at our parents' farm would never have worked."

"We tried it, but it was crowded, and their farm wasn't large enough to support us, and so it seemed coming here was our best hope." She stopped talking, and tears started forming at the corners of her eyes. "Whatever happened to those days in Tariverde? We had a nice life there. Those despicable people have ruined everything."

Johanna didn't have to ask who those people were. "Well, you're here, and I'm sure with your help the farm will provide everything we need, and we'll make it almost as good as home."

Elsa looked around as if she were taking in the whole house while sitting there at the table. "It's a lovely place, and this house is beyond nice. I'm so happy for you."

"It's large enough for all, and we're glad to share it."

Elsa got a thoughtful expression. "And the people who lived here before? What do you know of them?"

"Immediately before us were the Hubers. We never met them, but everyone says they were a nice couple."

"And German, from their name?"

"Yes."

"And before the Hubers?"

Johanna took in a deep breath. "No one has ever talked about those people."

Elsa rested her chin on her fist, her index finger along her cheek, something she'd always done when she was being thoughtful. "They were Czech, I would imagine."

"Most likely."

Both women grew quiet, imagining what might have befallen the family who preceded the Hubers, doubting their departure was a willing one.

"You've never asked, then?"

"No, the timing has never seemed right to do that. It might be a delicate conversation. It might open wounds. Things are good, so there's no need."

"That makes sense. And the other families here are Czech as well?"

"They are."

"And there is no resentment of your being German."

"They know our home was Dobrogea and not Germany, so that helps some I think, but the main thing that binds us is the farm. Everyone is committed to it, and that bridges any gap."

———————

In the office, the two men were studying the map showing the plan for the summer ahead. Herman thought it the best way to introduce the farm to Detlef, and based on the number of questions, it appeared he was correct. With all those questions, the conversation continued until it had grown late and was time for bed. The men headed to the kitchen, where their wives were waiting.

———

The long winter gave way to spring, and the cycle of life on the farm resumed. Johanna liked having Elsa there—another set of hands to help was always good, especially if those hands belonged to her sister. When the day's work was done and everyone was seated around the table, there was the sense of being back home in Romania.

But there were some complications from having another German family in the big house. During the previous year, Katerina and Johanna had settled into a comfortable routine. Katerina could anticipate what needed doing, and she knew when and how to involve the other women, but now with Johanna's sister there, would Elsa take Katerina's place as the second woman in charge? Would there be tasks she had performed that Elsa would now do? How would it all work?

Elsa, too, had questions. She didn't want to cause complications. At the same time, she didn't want to be just a guest. Johanna and Herman had been the last hope for her family, and she wanted to repay their graciousness by carrying her part of the load.

After a couple of weeks of awkwardness, Elsa went to her sister and asked her to sit down with her and Katerina and lay out how things should work. Johanna had sensed the discomfort of the two women and thought a conversation would be timely, so she seized the opportunity one day when the three of them were in the kitchen together. "Please sit, you two. We need to talk."

Katerina's brow knitted. "Is something wrong?"

"No, not at all." Johanna waited for them to take their seats before continuing. "Now that we've been together for a few weeks, I thought it might be good to talk about how we can best work together."

Elsa looked at Katerina to see how she was taking this, but there was no expression to read other than complete attention to what Johanna was saying.

"Katerina, you and I have a good partnership. You have been invaluable in making the other women part of our team, and I appreciate you so much for that. I want things to continue as they were before." She gestured toward Elsa. "But we now have another person to help us here, and we need to sort out how that will work. It will take time, but we will figure it out, and by this time next year, Elsa will have gone through every season on the farm and know exactly how she can help. Until then, she is willing to do whatever you or I need her to do."

Elsa looked at Katerina. "I want to help without getting in the way, so when it's not obvious what needs doing, I'll depend on you and Johanna to tell me."

Katerina's expression was a mix of relief and surprise. "Perfect. We can certainly use your help around here, and I know we will make a good team."

One day in late April, the two women were working in the kitchen along with Johanna. As a sign of their improving relationship, Katerina had the courage to ask Elsa about her life prior to coming to Strednitz, and Elsa, after a moment's hesitation, proceeded to tell her. Of course, much of the first part of Elsa's account—the time in Romania and the forced removal by the Nazis—was like the story of Johanna and Herman.

Johanna listened attentively as her sister talked of those years. The Detlef Elsa described was not exactly the Detlef Johanna knew; his shortcomings were unmentioned or glossed over, and his good moments received a disproportionate amount of attention. But who could blame her? Love always overlooks faults.

Elsa's expression grew darker as she said, "And there was the terrible day he was hurt."

Katerina asked her if she wanted to talk about that day, and Elsa said she did.

"He was standing in the rear of a truck, getting ready to step back to the dock, when the driver misunderstood a signal and pulled forward, leaving space between the back of the truck and the loading dock. Detlef lost his balance and fell in the gap. He caught his arm on the dock, breaking it and injuring his shoulder, then fell to the ground, breaking a bone in his leg and injuring his back. He lay there, and his supervisor came to the edge of the dock and yelled at him for being careless. Finally, when he didn't get up, one of his fellow workers convinced the supervisor that Detlef was badly hurt. He was unable to walk, and it hurt too much when they tried to help him, so they found a chair for him to sit in, then carried him—chair and all—to an office. He was directed to seek medical care and told not to report back until he was better. They told him that he certainly should not expect a paycheck until he returned.

"Someone came to the house to let me know, and I went to see him. When I arrived, he was in so much pain and so battered, I wanted to cry. But

I was too angry, so I yelled at the men who were standing there looking at us. Needless to say, that didn't help our standing. I had come with our horse and wagon, and once we had loaded Detlef in it, I drove the streets looking to get him help. He hurt so much he passed out, and I was afraid he might die before we found help. We tried to find a hospital that would see us, but the first one refused, and we had to travel to another farther away." Elsa's voice broke as she continued, "If we could have gotten him care earlier, I'm sure he would be better off than he is now." Elsa now had tears in her eyes.

Katerina put her hand on Elsa's shoulder. "It must have been awful."

"It was. We tried to get him well so that he could return to work, but it was a long process, and no one wanted to employ a damaged man. As I said, he earned no paycheck after his injury, but we received some help from neighbors and friends and even some assistance from a few of his co-workers. Finally we exhausted our savings and the help disappeared." She looked at Johanna before continuing. "We contacted our parents and went to live on their little farm near Dresden, but their house was small and we were too much for them. It was then we contacted dear Johanna, and here we are, thanks to her and Herman, with a wonderful place to stay until Detlef recovers."

Johanna patted her sister's hand. "And you would have done the same for us."

"Yes, of course we would have."

Katerina said, "Your Detlef seems to be doing better. Maybe the good air of Czechoslovakia agrees with him."

"I'm sure it does, and a family's love is healing, as well."

––––––––––

At the same time out in the fields, the men had started planting oats and barley. Detlef was among them. He had proven to be helpful, but Herman noticed a pattern in which his injuries became more troublesome on days when the work was particularly difficult. On some of those days, he would be late getting to wherever the men were working, and on others, his pain would force him to quit early. The other men noticed, and when Herman wasn't around, they talked about it. Marek noted that Detlef seemed to move a little more freely when he thought no one was watching. Filip told him to be quiet, because the man was nearly the brother of Herman, and they should be more respectful.

"Well, he should be respectful of us as well."

"Marek, need I remind you that we live and work here at the discretion of the Muellers? It's always the right thing to be respectful of others, but it's especially prudent in our situation."

Marek's expression indicated compliance but not agreement.

On an afternoon two days later, Herman walked into the middle of a heated conversation between Detlef and Filip. Detlef had his back to Herman and didn't see him coming.

"And please don't forget, Filip, that I am Herman's brother-in-law, and I'm sure he would agree with my suggestion."

Herman reached the men. "What suggestion would I agree with, Detlef?"

"I'm suggesting some improvements to this year's plan. I think we can make more money if we implement them."

"What might those be?"

"I think we should grow some additional sugar beets. They did well last year."

"I see."

"You don't agree?"

"Detlef, there's a short-term benefit to that, but it might not be as good for the farm in the long run."

His cheeks growing red, Detlef said, "So you're not even going to consider my suggestion?"

"Not at this time, no. Filip knows this farm, and he has a good plan for it. We need to stay with it. I'm sure you see why I think that's the best approach."

"I see that you feel that way and you are the master of this place. So . . ."

"Detlef, we can always look at the plan this fall. That would be a better time to consider alterations and adjustments." He turned to the Czech. "Wouldn't you agree, Filip?"

"I'd be happy to hear all ideas then, and we can make any changes at that time."

Detlef, seeing everyone's eyes on him and wanting to regain lost ground, accepted their offer of compromise. "Very well. I'll be ready to talk when you are."

"Good. Rain's coming, men. Let's get back to work."

The two other Czechs had been watching the exchange, and although they only caught a word here and there, they could tell what had transpired. They knew Filip had been supported and the brother-in-law put in his place. They were pleased with both developments.

17

Summer and Fall

1943

Soon Annelise and Emma were home, and all the young ones were out of school. The children were looking forward to a vacation from schoolwork, but Herman and Johanna were convinced young Georg hadn't progressed all that much. Considering the number of teachers he'd had and his indifferent attitude toward learning, they were correct. They decided that Annelise should tutor her little brother in spelling and geography. Georg argued to no avail that he'd be needed in the fields, and Annelise wondered what she'd done to deserve the punishment of spending hours each morning working with such a reluctant learner.

Their parents were adamant, so a large map of the world was spread across the big table each morning and word lists prepared. Georg proved to be a willing student where geography was concerned, but he was less successful at spelling. When it was time for those lessons, he grew restless and became something of a problem for his sister. It went on for a few days, until Annelise complained to their father that Georg wasn't cooperating. Herman told her she had all the rights and privileges of a teacher. She brightened at this and had no hesitation to administer punishment to the boy.

When the hired girls came to the farm in late May, six of the eight were returnees. They would be a great help, but there was always the possibility that they could make life on the farm more complicated.

It was obvious to everyone that at least a couple of the girls were infatuated with Marek Czerný, and he didn't mind their attention in the least. On one occasion, Marek got into a play-fight with Rolf. He jokingly tossed a bucket of water on Rolf, and later the boy snuck up on him and returned the favor. Marek's shirt got soaked, so he took it off to wring it out. It was an instinctive move, but there were girls around to admire his physique. Enjoying that attention, he was very deliberate about putting his shirt back on.

Filip scolded him for it, saying that going shirtless was okay for boys but not for a married man. When the scolding was finished, Marek turned and grinned at the girls, and a couple of them snickered. One's eyes lingered on him, and Marek caught her staring.

There came a warm night when Marek's wife and two children were asleep, and he sat outside looking at the stars and enjoying the breeze as he had done several nights in a row. The dormitory was just up the hill from the Czernýs' home, so the girls had noticed Marek's evening routine. That night, the girl who'd eyed him came out, and she saw Marek sitting there alone, his shirt unbuttoned and his hands behind his head.

There were two versions of what happened next. Hers was that Marek lured her and then tried to have his way with her. His version was that she came to him, flirted with him, tried to kiss him, then touched him, hoping to arouse his interest.

All that was known for sure was that at one point the girl started yelling out in a loud voice, waking Marek's wife and the Dvoráks. The girl was screaming hysterically by that point and had to be comforted by Teresa Dvorák, who took her back up the hill to the dormitory. Jan Dvorák stayed to talk to Marek and his wife. Veronica had come outside to see what was going on, and she was upset about the situation. She knew her husband was a man that women found attractive, and she wasn't sure he'd always been faithful. She stood there stone-faced, listening to Marek's pleading and wanting to believe him. After all, even as foolish as Marek could be, it was unlikely that he would have chosen a spot outside the door of their home to have his way with a girl. More to the point, Veronica knew if the allegations were true, then they would have to leave the farm and be left with no home and no employment, so she thought it prudent to let Marek know that she believed him.

Seeing his wife take his side, Marek turned his protesting to Dvorák and his wife, who had just returned from the dormitory. They listened without emotion, and their stoicism angered him. He started to say ugly things about the girl. Jan Dvorák tried to calm him, telling Marek his anger wouldn't help. Veronica took his hands in hers and told him to calm down, repeating that she believed him. When she repeated her support, Marek grew quiet, and Jan Dvorák witnessed something he never imagined he'd see. There was a look of gratitude in young Marek's eyes.

Dvořák told the young man they would talk with Filip about it in the morning, and he would decide the matter. They all knew that Filip wasn't fond of Marek, and he might take the matter to Herman, and if Herman believed the girl, then the Czernýs might be forced to leave the farm. They were quiet as they went to their homes that night.

The next day, Filip met with Jan and Marek. After listening to their accounts of the previous evening, he told them that before he troubled Herman with it, he wanted to interview the girl. Marek was surprised by this, and for that matter, so was Dvořák, but Filip Novák was a fair man, and they understood that talking to the girl was what a fair man should do.

Filip had the girl meet him outside Dvořák's home, with Mrs. Dvořák there. Since she'd heard much of what happened the night before, he thought she might help with the conversation.

He got straight to the point. "So there was a problem last night between you and Marek Czerný."

"Yes, there was. He was terrible to me."

"Can you tell us about it?"

"Do I have to?" She started crying. "I don't really want to think about it."

"Well, if he did something wrong, we need to know, and we can't know if you don't tell us."

Between sniffles, she whispered, "He tried to . . ."

Teresa said, "Have his way with you?"

"Yes."

Filip looked at Mrs. Dvořák, his expression telling her not to put words in the girl's mouth. "Where was this?"

"At his house."

"Inside?"

"No, outside."

"What were you doing at his house?"

"I stepped outside for some fresh air. It was hot in our dormitory, and he was waiting by his door. He asked me to come down and sit with him. He said it was a nice evening and his wife was asleep and he wanted someone to talk to."

Filip's brow wrinkled as he considered her words. "Did you not think it inappropriate to go to a married man's house?"

E.N. Klinginsmith

"He's always been nice to me when we work together. I just thought of him as a friend."

"So this friend is a man a few years older than you, with a wife and two small children, and you thought it was a good thing to do to go to his house and talk with him?"

"It was a nice night outside. I liked the idea of talking with him. I know now it was wrong. I just didn't think."

"Okay, and then what happened?"

"We talked . . ."

"For how long?"

She looked surprised. "For how long?"

"Yes, how long did you and Marek Czerný sit outside his house, with his wife sleeping inside, and talk?"

She was flustered by that. "I don't know. It wasn't long. We talked for a minute, and then he tried to kiss me. I pushed him away, then he grabbed me and pulled me close to him."

Filip tilted his head. "And with his wife only a few meters away, he did all this?"

She gave Filip an angry look. "You don't believe me! I should have known a man would take Marek's side."

"Forgive me, but it's hard to believe. I would think if a man wanted to kiss or make love to a girl, he wouldn't choose to do it by his home with his wife asleep inside."

She turned to Teresa. "Dvoráková, you believe me, don't you?"

Teresa gave the girl a kind look. "It's not for me to say, dear. But I will say, even as a young girl, I would know better than to go sit by a married man after dark, even to talk. You say you consider him a friend, but it isn't something a girl should do."

"So you don't believe me!"

"I am saying you should not have gone there in the first place. That's all."

The girl stood up. "Then I guess I'm left with no choice. I should leave the farm!"

If the girl was bluffing, she didn't get the response she wanted. Filip simply said, "I think that would be for the best."

Teresa's eyes widened, but she said nothing.

"I can tell you this, for sure. My father will be here soon after I go home, and he won't be happy with how I've been treated."

Filip said, "Then he should talk with me, but let me warn you that if he tries to start something with Marek, there'll be trouble, and it will be trouble that he won't want to have."

She tried another tactic. "I'm going to tell all the girls what's just happened here, and I think they may want to leave, too, if I have to leave."

That was something Filip had considered. "Then let's talk with one of them to see what she has to say."

With another bluff called, the girl backed down. "No! Forget it! I'll let my father deal with it."

The girl left soon after the conversation, and the next day, as she'd predicted, her father came to the farm demanding to see Filip Novák.

Georg ran to the field to get him, and Filip came to the house bringing two of the summer girls with him.

"Filip Novák?"

"Yes. That's me."

"I'm not happy with you. My daughter was badly treated by one of the men on the farm, the one who goes around taking off his shirt and showing off his muscles to the girls. The one who calls girls to sit with him, then tries to take advantage, and you've taken his side."

"I think what your daughter has told you isn't the whole story."

"Is that so?"

"Did she tell you the incident happened outside the Czernýs' house with the young man's wife and children on the other side of the door?"

"She did, and that's why she thought she could trust him to behave himself."

"And you think her going to the house of a married man that night was an appropriate thing for a young woman to do?"

"I've told her it wasn't. Still, it's not the girl's fault that he tried to force himself on her."

At this point, one of the girls spoke up. "We don't think he did that."

The angry father turned on her. "And how do you know? Were you there?"

"I wasn't." She looked at the other girl, then said, "We weren't, but your daughter has had eyes for Marek since she got here, and she's made no secret how handsome she thinks he is and how . . ."

"And how what?"

"And how she wouldn't object to a show of affection."

The father's voice rose even higher. "What! I don't believe that."

The other girl spoke up. "It's true. She has a girl's crush on him, and we've told her it's silly. He's married, and there's no future. Still there are nights when the rest of us are trying to get to sleep, she talks of little else."

Filip looked at the girl's father and said, "The other girls will support what these two say. I won't deny that Marek likes to show off to the girls, and I've reprimanded him for that, but I don't believe he called your daughter over to his house. I think she went there to flirt with him, and when he didn't return her interest, her feelings were hurt. Her embarrassment became anger, and she started yelling at him. That got the attention of the Dvoráks and Marek's wife, Veronica, and when they came to see what was going on, she couldn't think of any other way to get out of the situation than to blame Marek."

"Hmmpf! That version works very nicely for your young man, doesn't it?"

Filip squared himself and looked directly at the man. "So you're thinking I'm not telling you the truth?"

The father, knowing his daughter and sensing the battle was lost, said, "No. I believe you. She can be a silly girl at times, as all girls can. I've heard you're a good man, Filip Novák. I suppose the other girls and the young man have told you the truth, and you are doing the same with me."

Filip's expression softened at that, and he said, "Thank you for saying that. I try to be honest, and I always seek to be fair."

"So what do we do now? May she return to the farm? We're a poor family, and what she would earn this summer would help us."

This part was difficult for Filip. As far as he could tell, the young woman had told a lie, one that could have caused a problem for Marek and his wife. It wasn't a minor situation. Filip was himself the parent of three daughters, and he wanted to be kind to the girl, but she had caused too much trouble already.

He sighed. "I think it is in the best interest of everyone that she doesn't return. We will calculate what we owe her and make settlement with you at summer's end."

The man was devastated. "If that's how it will be, then I guess there isn't any reason for me to remain."

The man walked slowly down the hill to the main road. He had a long walk home, and an unhappy one that day. He had the look of a man who, on top of everything else, would have an upset wife when he got home. Filip almost went after the man to save him that trouble and to help his family out, but the decision had been made.

Word of the encounter traveled quickly. The other girls were upset because one less girl meant more work for them. Beyond that, she was just a foolish girl who'd gotten carried away, and she deserved a lesser punishment. Finally, they thought that Marek, with his flirtatiousness and his showing off in front of them, should bear some of the blame. Still, the girls wouldn't cause problems over this. They needed their jobs.

That night, Marek told his wife the outcome, and surprisingly Veronica expressed sympathy for the girl. She knew what the loss of the job would mean for the girl's family.

The Muellers were the last to hear of the incident. When he was told of it, Herman thought Filip had done the right thing, but Johanna disagreed, thinking the girl should have been given another chance. The next evening, after the children had left the table, Herman, Johanna, Elsa, and Detlef remained, enjoying some of Johanna's coffee before retiring for the night. Elsa weighed in on the matter, saying she thought the girl was treated unfairly, and Detlef voiced his agreement. Herman listened for a while, then raised his hand with his palm toward them. "It's enough about this. A decision has been made, and we'll not speak of it anymore."

As the other couple went up for the night, Herman and Johanna could hear Detlef saying, in a voice he thought only Elsa could hear, "I think the decision should not have been Filip's. There are times he forgets his place here."

Herman shook his head and whispered, "He might not be the only one."

Johanna could tell her husband had nearly lost his patience with Detlef, and she looked down at her hands, trying to think of what she could say or do to make things better. Herman, seeing her distress and knowing Johanna was in a difficult position, went to her and put his arm around her. "But it will be okay."

———

A few days later, the father returned with the girl and asked to see Filip again. When word reached him, Filip started toward the house, and Herman accompanied him, wanting to put an end to this situation. When the father saw Herman with Filip, he had difficulty getting his words out, and when he finally finished saying his piece, Filip translated it for Herman. "He says he's here today because his daughter wishes to apologize to Czerna for the trouble she caused in her marriage."

Herman said, "That won't be necessary," and Filip translated Herman's words.

The father wrung his hands and begged, "Please sir, it's the right thing for her to do. At least give us that."

As Filip was translating, another voice was heard. "Let her do it, Herman." The four of them turned to see that Johanna had come outside, and she'd been listening to the conversation.

Herman could tell by her tone that he should listen to Johanna. "Okay. Filip, tell the man that we'll let his daughter apologize to Mrs. Czerný." Filip translated, and the man showed his appreciation by shaking Filip's hand. The girl gave Johanna a shy smile as her way of saying thanks.

Johanna continued, "And Mrs. Novák and I will go with them, just to make sure all goes well."

Herman and Filip knew their wives would handle the situation, so they agreed. Filip translated for the man and his daughter, and they waited for Johanna to get Katerina Novák.

Later that evening, once again the four adults were gathered at the table. Johanna told the others how the conversation had gone, and that Veronica Czerný had forgiven the girl for causing a problem.

Herman nodded. "That was kind of her."

Then Johanna added, "There was one more thing I promised that I would do."

"You made a promise?"

She looked directly at Herman and said, "Yes, I promised that I would persuade you to bring the girl back to the farm. She made a mistake, and it was an unfortunate one, but the price she's paying is too heavy. Her family needs what her work here will earn. They need more than the partial payment they've been promised."

"But Marek . . . he'll . . ."

Johanna raised her hand. "His wife is determined this should happen, and she has assured us Marek will be fine with it."

Herman smiled. "Veronica's going to ensure that he's fine?"

Johanna laughed. "Yes, and if you'd seen the look on her face, you'd have no doubt."

That got a laugh from the rest.

"And Filip? We're going against his decision."

Detlef weighed in. "He needs to do what you say, Herman."

Herman glared at Detlef, and Elsa spoke up. "Detlef, stay out of this. We're guests. Appreciate what we have and stop putting your nose in where it isn't wanted."

Johanna smiled at her sister's remark, then turned to face her husband. "His wife will make sure Filip is okay with this, so it is left to you, Herman."

"Okay then. This is what we'll do. Have Mrs. Novák deliver the message to the family, letting them know the girl can return. I'll see that Filip has a conversation with Marek to make sure he understands how things are, and to make sure he watches himself around the girls."

"He is quite good-looking."

They laughed because Elsa was the last one they'd expect to say something like that.

Two days later the girl returned, and the summer went quickly from there, with only the normal difficulties of life on a farm. Within a month, the days grew shorter and the work began to slow. The summer girls were paid as they left for their homes. Not long after that, Annelise and Emma left for school in Prague, with Rolf joining them. Georg made the daily trip to his school in Vysoka. The Czech children attended the same school as he, but they accompanied their friends and classmates, leaving him to make the trip alone most days. He missed his older brother.

With the youngsters gone it was quiet once again at #1 Strednitz. Still there was work to be done. After the crops were harvested, the vegetables were canned and stored, and three hogs were butchered once more. Autumn flew by and winter took hold.

———

Another Christmas came, and Annelise got the skis she'd wished for a year earlier, as did Rolf. Georg was thought to be too young for a pair, and he did a poor job of hiding his disappointment. Rolf fashioned a couple of saplings into crude skis so he could join them. Cousin Emma showed little interest, so it was the three Mueller youngsters who skied on the hills of the farm.

Georg wasn't bad for a little boy with makeshift skis. Rolf, older and with better equipment, was a satisfactory skier, but Annelise surpassed them both. With each run she improved, and within a couple of days she looked as if she had skied for years. Her brothers marveled at her grace and skill.

Then came the day before she was to return to school—a sunny, chilly day with fresh snow on the hillside, feathery and perfect for skiing. The three of them hurried through breakfast, hardly tasting a bite of their food, and headed for their favorite hill. Annelise made several passes, carving out a path that slid past the rough spots and skirted the few trees on the hill. As lunchtime approached, she stood at the top of the hill, ready for one last run, and she challenged herself to make it her best one of the morning.

She pushed from her starting point, then flexed her knees so that they could absorb the few rough spots ahead. She hadn't gone far when she saw Georg starting to walk across her path at the bottom of the hill. She focused on him, calculating her route to make sure she didn't collide with him. Her lack of attention proved costly. A small tree she'd negotiated a dozen times that morning loomed ahead of her, and by the time she remembered it, she couldn't correct her course. She yelled as she neared it, and Georg looked up the slope at his sister. He saw her put her hands out to protect herself, but her speed was too great, and she caught it first with her hands, then with her torso and face. It wasn't a large tree, but it was sturdy enough to halt her progress, knocking her to her seat with her skis straddling it. She felt the sting of a split lip, but her wounded pride was worse.

Rolf skied to her and helped her up. Once up, she skied to the bottom of the hill and gave Georg a glare, then, with her skis under her arms, she headed to the house. Rolf finished his run, then yelled at Georg, "This is all your fault. Why were you not paying attention?"

Georg felt the double humiliation of seeing his sister hurt while being blamed for it by his older brother. He picked up his skis and walked silently to the house a few steps behind Rolf, who seemed to want nothing to do with him. When the boys got inside, they removed their coats and boots, then walked to the kitchen where they saw Johanna tending to Annelise's lip. She looked up and scowled at her boys as they entered, her look letting them know that she was unhappy. Annelise was crying, not only about the injury but because she would be returning to Prague with a swollen lip that she'd have to explain to her friends. They might question her ability to ski, and there'd be no way for her to prove them wrong.

Annelise never skied again after that day, and Georg carried the guilt of that with him, reminded of it every time he saw fresh snow on the hills.

❦ 18 ❧

The Turning Tide

January 1944

Not long after Annelise and the others had returned to Prague, the sun rose on an unseasonably warm morning. The snow that had made for good skiing started to melt, but by late afternoon the weather changed, the clouds came in, and snow started falling again. It continued overnight and for two more days. Life became more difficult on the farm, with the deep snow making even simple tasks a chore. The cheerfulness of the holiday season was a memory, and spring was a long way off, but knowing it would come one day helped get them through.

Something felt different though, and it wasn't just the abnormally heavy snow cover. Word had begun to spread through both the Czech and German communities that the tide of war was turning. Listening to the German reports on the radio gave a much different impression, but the Muellers, like the other German families, had long since grown skeptical of such news.

More than once Herman caught the three Czech men whispering among themselves, no doubt sharing reports and rumors they'd heard. When Herman asked them if something was wrong, there were sheepish expressions and assurances things were fine; they were only exchanging village gossip. He knew what it was they were discussing, and it was another reminder that he was a German man on a farm in the middle of Bohemia.

Signs began to appear that confirmed things had changed. German soldiers who were headed to the Eastern Front started coming through the village. Many of them stopped at the farm for a home-cooked meal and a night's rest before moving on. From the way the men talked, it was obvious they were rushing to the front to help halt the Russian advance.

Georg adored the soldiers. After all, he was a seven-year-old boy, the uniformed men carried weapons, and any little boy would be impressed by that. One pair took him out to an open field and let him fire a round with one of their weapons. Johanna wasn't enthusiastic about it, but Herman saw no problem, but only that night. For Georg it was great fun standing out there, firing off into the distance, hearing the report of the gun, and bracing himself against its recoil. The next day the men left for the front. From then on, weapons being fired were something altogether different than standing out in a field with a little boy.

The Czechs kept their distance and remained quiet for days after the soldiers had come through. They continued to work hard as usual, and when they were in the fields things seemed almost normal, but their silence spoke of their unhappiness with the soldiers of the Reich.

Sometimes when there were numerous soldiers in need of a place to stay overnight, they would be sent to the girls' dormitory. There was a small woodstove there, and while it barely warmed the space, at least the men were inside and out of the weather—a luxury they wouldn't have once they reached the front.

A few of them spoke of their devotion to Germany and their belief in the cause. They were the ones who'd say "Heil Hitler" when they left. Little Georg was usually the only one to return it, unless the look on the men's faces told Herman he was expected to return it as well. Even then, his was a perfunctory salute. Johanna simply smiled and wished the soldiers a safe return to their families.

Most of the men seemed unexcited or worried about what lay ahead, and they simply thanked the Muellers for their hospitality, then said their farewells. Johanna would stand on the porch watching them leave, worried for their safety and lamenting the waste of it all. She had received word that Rolf had felt compelled to join the Hitler Youth at school, and she disliked the thought of him becoming one of the young men she watched come and go.

One visitor proved to be more informative than the others. After the rest of his band had gone to the dormitory, he stayed to join Herman on the porch. The young man borrowed Herman's pipe to light a cigarette. He had promised his mother he'd quit, and he felt smoking in front of Johanna was a violation of his promise. Between drags, he told Herman how far west the front had moved and that there could be a time that even Bohemia might no longer be under German control.

"The Allies are in Italy now, and there is talk that in spite of the German defenses they will attempt to land somewhere in France." Then the young man, having gotten as much out of his cigarette as he could, stubbed it out and said, "It will be like a vise on Germany when that happens." He stopped, and the meaning of all he had just said was written on his young face. "I think the war is not going to end well for us, and I worry that I may never see my parents again."

"Let's hope you're wrong there. I know they miss you and that they pray for your return, so you need to do everything you can to make it home to them. You need to answer their prayers."

"That would be God's work, I suppose. Or will it be left to the Fates perhaps?"

As he looked at the young man, Herman couldn't help but think of Peter's sons. Already his oldest had been reported missing and was presumed captured or dead, and news came slowly from the others. It was worrisome to say the least. And then the Pöhlmanns had gotten the devastating news that their beloved Fritz hadn't survived his wounds. Their loss was unbearable, and there were days they hardly moved, sitting in the kitchen staring at each other, neither able to help with the other's grief. Herman and Johanna called on them as often as they could. It helped while they were there, but they knew as soon as they left, the weight of their loss would weigh on Günter and Olexa once again.

The young man shoved his hands in his coat pockets and, avoiding eye contact, said, "You may not be completely safe yourself."

"From the Russians?"

"No, from being called into service. They're drafting younger men, and then even younger men, and the only move left is to draft older ones such as you. You're young enough, and even here in Strednitz, I think they may find you."

Herman thought that might be possible. When they moved to Strednitz, he and Ritter made sure the papers were in order to take possession of the farm. Now that compliance could allow the Nazis to locate him. He tried to dismiss the thought as quickly as it came on, thinking that even if they started drafting men in their thirties, he was forty, and he should be safe. Still it troubled him.

As Herman was thinking, the boy got a wistful smile and said, "But I have another reason to be safe in addition to my parents."

"And what is that?"

"We were delayed in Austria." The smile broadened.

"I suspect I might know why."

"On what was to be our last night there, we met a group of young women, and they caused our delay. Some of them were quite attractive, but it didn't matter if they were or not. They were girls and they were . . . accommodating. The one I spent time with was beautiful and quite friendly to me." He got an even bigger smile, then continued, "Because of her, I have another reason to survive this war. I want to go back and find her, and I'll make her my wife, I think."

Herman had a thought he didn't share, which was that the girl may have been friends with other soldiers moving east and might befriend more men in the days ahead. But what would be the point of his saying that? The boy had had his first taste of love, and who was Herman to take that away from him? The boy was heading into a hellish war in late winter. Let him have his memory and his dreams. He needed something to be fighting for, and fighting for the memory of a girl's embrace was certainly better than fighting for whatever cause the Nazis proclaimed. Herman wanted the boy to survive and hoped he'd find that girl, and the two of them would make a life together, with a house full of children to raise.

———

The tide of men continued as the spring came on, and thoughts of what might lay ahead were always on the minds of the Muellers. Still they proceeded to do what needed to be done, because day-to-day farm activities were things within their control, and as practical people it was better to put their thoughts and efforts there.

On the way to school one morning, Georg found strips of foil spread all over the ground. He gathered some of the strips to take with him, and when he got to school, the other kids had found some, too, and there was noisy chatter in the classroom as they tried to figure out where they'd come from and what their purpose was. Some wondered if the foil strips had something to do with the planes they'd heard the night before. The children showed them to the young teacher and asked her if she had an idea what they might be. She had no answers, suggesting they ask their parents when they got home.

Georg had trouble paying attention that day. The bright strips of foil on his desk were interesting, and he couldn't wait to get home to ask his parents about them. When they were dismissed he dashed home and went directly to his mother. He showed her the strips and told her that they were spread throughout the area. She looked at them for a moment, and she, too, was puzzled. She thought perhaps his father might know, so Georg went to find him.

He found his father out near the barn and asked him about the foil. Herman had seen a few pieces around the farm that day, and he speculated that they could be from the planes since the foil had only started appearing when the planes had begun to fly overhead. Other than that, he had no idea what the strips were for.

The next day, the kids had found more foil on their way to school, and they shared their parents' opinions. Again, planes had been heard the night before, so there must be some connection. But why would planes, machines of war, drop bright strips of aluminum? Some of the kids were wary of the strips, but Georg was intrigued, and he continued to hold on to the ones he'd found, adding them to the collection in his room.

That night, another group of soldiers showed up at the Mueller home, and one of them put an end to the mystery. "You've had planes flying overhead."

Herman looked at the soldier sitting across from him and said, "Yes, and how do you know that?"

"We've seen the foil on the ground, and the foil tells us about the planes."

Herman leaned toward the man and asked, "What does the foil tell you about the planes?"

"Let me ask you a question. What is it the pilots and crews fear most?"

"Being shot down, of course."

"And what time of day do planes fly in order to lessen the chances of their being spotted and shot down?"

"At night."

"Exactly, and what helps the gunners find those planes in the dark, so that they can take them out of the skies before they do their damage?"

Herman leaned back into his chair, thought about it for a moment, then responded, "That would be radar, I would imagine."

"Exactly. What we've been told is that the planes release bales of aluminum strips, and those strips fill the air. The radar, instead of seeing a few planes, displays hundreds of images, so the shooting cannot be directed at specific targets. Thus more enemy planes make it to their destinations, and more damage is done. So the bright strips of aluminum have a sinister purpose."

"I see."

Georg overheard the conversation. He was excited to have an answer, and he couldn't wait to get to school to share what he knew. To make sure he was right, he'd check with his father first, but the next day couldn't come fast enough.

In the days that followed, more and more soldiers came through the farm, and some older men were among them. One such man was with a group of soldiers who jokingly referred to him as their Opa. He returned their teasing, calling them welpen. When Herman asked his age, the man replied he was thirty-five, married, and the father of two. Johanna asked the ages of his children. "My boy is twelve and our daughter, eleven." The man looked at the floor as if his shoes held something of interest, then said, "I thought I was safe from being called, what with my age and the two children. Still they came for me." He looked at Herman but said nothing. His message had already been delivered.

After the men had gone to bed, Herman helped Johanna clear the table and put things away. As they stood in the kitchen, he said, "It appears my day may be coming, so we need to start talking about how things will be on the farm if and when I'm not here."

"None of that talk. I won't let them take you!"

"You won't have a say in it, nor will I. If they come for me, I'll have to go."

She wrapped her arms around his waist and leaned her head against his chest, breathing in the smell of him. And then, as hard as she tried not to, she couldn't help but sob, her tears dampening his shirt. "You can't leave us. We have three children and this farm. I need you here with me. We all do. This would be so wrong. I don't want you putting your life in danger for the dog-killers."

He put his hand under her chin and tilted her face so that she was looking at him. "This is wartime, and everything is turned upside down now, and that which should never happen does so more and more. War is a time when ordinary men, good men with loving families, are being sent to fight the battles of weak-minded cowards in guarded sanctuaries who have their families and their cronies with them, safe from harm. But that's nothing new in times of war. It's been that way for centuries, and I'm afraid I'll soon be one of the ordinary men chosen to fight the battles of the ones who've caused all this—the ones who killed our dogs and took our home from us."

She leaned into him again. "Still, I don't want to talk about it. It's as if our planning for it will make it so."

"We have to be prepared, dear."

She held him even tighter, thinking they could never take him from her if she wouldn't let go of him. He took the back of his hand and brushed it against her cheek, then she took hers and held his hand there. She looked up at him again, tears still flowing, and he kissed her forehead.

"We need to have this talk whether we want to or not."

She relented and asked him to tell her his thoughts.

"I'll want Filip to run the farm. He knows everything about it, and he's good with the other men. Filip is the best one to manage things when it's my time to go."

"If you go."

"If I go, then."

Johanna thought such an arrangement might pose a problem with Detlef. He'd most likely think that as the remaining German man on the farm, he should be placed in charge. She shared her concern with Herman.

Herman listened to her and said, "Okay. To leave no doubt, I'll sit down with the two of them tomorrow and tell them how it will be. Detlef needs to accept this if he chooses to stay here."

"What would be my place in this arrangement?"

"Your place?"

"I'm a woman. With you gone, our place here might be tenuous, especially if it appears Germany is in danger of being defeated."

"I'll suggest that Filip report to you each day. He'll keep things going, but I think it's only proper that he communicate with you."

"You think so?"

"You know more about the farm than you think you do. You'll have good questions, and I'm sure you'll have suggestions that might help him, but of equal importance, my requiring him to report to you will serve as a subtle reminder to Filip the farm isn't his just yet."

She stepped back and put both hands on his chest. "You think a woman can handle this?"

He took her hands in his, holding them against him. "I think you can. After everything you've been through these last five years, I think you'll do fine. In fact, I know you will."

"Well, I don't want to do this alone, but you've convinced me it would be good for you to talk with Filip and Detlef, and then when they have heard your plan and agreed to it, the three of you can tell the other two about the arrangement. It would remove any chance that Detlef will try to assume leadership, and for a time at least, it should allow us to continue to live here."

Herman smiled. "See, this is what I was saying. You know what needs to be done. Don't doubt yourself."

"Still, Herman, I pray you'll never leave me."

To stay there on the farm with her, the children, and the others was the thing he most wanted in the world. He wanted to feel that the two of them would be more than a match for anything the Nazis would do to them, but as he stood there holding her close, he thought back to those days in Tariverde when they'd believed they could stand up against the Nazis. He knew there was a chance things could go just as badly, if not worse, and he knew he could either comply or risk the repercussions.

The next day Herman held that conversation with the men, and their agreement was made. Detlef was quiet at first, then asked, "What shall we do if Filip is not available and some decision needs to be made?"

Herman knew Detlef was probing for some small opportunity to insert himself into a position of leadership. "I think you need to make sure that times like that never happen."

Detlef pushed for his answer. "But should I take charge in such an eventuality?"

"Well, let me ask you this: How would you tell the other men what you want them to do in such a situation, Detlef?"

Detlef was a bit flustered. He realized that all communication with Jan and Marek flowed through Filip, and that weakened his case. "Those men should know some German already, and if not, they need to learn some basic phrases. It's time!"

Herman countered his argument. "You have more education than they do, Detlef, and I'm sure Filip would be a good teacher. Why don't we have him teach you some simple Czech phrases—a few each night. Then you could talk to them in their language and get done what needs to be done."

Filip tried hard not to show his amusement, knowing there was no way Detlef would take time to learn even the most basic Czech.

Detlef conceded, "No, you're right. Maybe it would be better if one of the other men is separated from us if the need arises, so the problem of not having Filip won't occur."

"Or you could be the one to go take care of things while the Czech men continue working."

Detlef's eyes darted from Herman to Filip, then back, and with no expression in his voice, he said, "Yes, that could work as well."

The discussion had reached its conclusion, and the other two men were summoned and informed of what had been decided. Jan Dvořák spoke when Filip finished, and Novák translated his words. "He says it's the wish of all of us that you will not be called away to serve in the German army."

Herman smiled in appreciation, knowing the odds were getting worse that their wish would be granted.

———

Only a few days later, a letter arrived informing Herman that he was being drafted into the army. He was not told a specific date, but the letter indicated that he and men like him in the area would soon be collected by officials and assigned to units. When he showed the letter to Johanna, she slumped into a chair and sat there silent and still. He'd expected an outburst of tears or anger or both, and for her to react as she did was almost worse.

He pulled up a chair and faced her, then took her hands, and when she looked at him, it was as if she was looking through him at a grim future for the two of them. He let her sit there, sorting out her thoughts, then said, "Well, we need to call the others in and tell them the news." At first it was as if she hadn't heard him, then her attention returned, and she nodded her agreement. He said, "I'll be back," then went to find Detlef and Filip.

He brought them into the office to tell them his news, and they did a poor job of showing their shock. It was one thing to think it might happen someday, yet another to know that day had nearly arrived. They told him they were sorry to hear his news, stood around nervously for a few more minutes, then shuffled out of the room. After that day, perhaps because they knew no other way to respond, they simply continued to go about daily business as they had always done, because when they were busy it was as though nothing bad could happen.

The day the official came to their house was eerily like the time in Tariverde when the uniformed men arrived and everything began to unravel. Johanna heard noise and went to the window to see what was going on. A man had pulled up on a motorcycle with an empty sidecar. Seeing that empty seat was an ominous sign. The man in uniform wasn't there to make a social call.

The knock on the door was rude and insistent. Elsa asked if she should get it, but Johanna said she'd answer. Mrs. Novák was standing there, taking it all in, a worried expression on her face.

Johanna opened the door. "May we help you?"

A man with cold blue eyes and an expressionless face said, "This is the home of Herman Mueller, is it not?"

"It is. May I ask what you want with my husband?"

"I would rather speak with him. Please go get him for me."

Johanna turned to Elsa, who nodded and then left to go to the field to fetch Herman.

"Please come in."

She seated the man in the windowed sitting room and asked him if he would like something to drink. He declined her offer, and somehow even that seemed menacing. He asked if he might smoke while he waited, and she found a dish for his ashes. He didn't seem like the type of man for small talk, and she hated the look and smell of him at this point, so she excused herself, letting him know Herman would join him shortly.

Georg was home that day, claiming illness. He'd been told to sit at the dining room table and work on his spelling and reading. When he heard his mother talking to the man in the other room, he stepped in to look at him. Johanna was leaving. She grabbed the boy by his arm and said, "Come, Georg, let's leave the man alone." Georg turned around to study the man as his mother walked him briskly out of the room.

As they made their way to the kitchen, Georg whispered, "I don't like that man."

"Shhh. He'll hear you."

In a softer whisper he said, "Well, I don't."

Soon they heard footsteps on the porch and the front door opening. Johanna came around to the mudroom and directed Herman to where the man was waiting, her words unneeded with the stale odor of the man's cigarettes giving him away. Herman gave her a gesture as if to say, "I'll take care of this. You wait here."

Herman walked through his office, past his desk with the planting plan spread out on it, and into the sitting room. When he came in, the uniformed man stood and extended his hand, and introductions were made.

That finished, Herman asked, "What do you need from me?"

"Herr Mueller, to get to the point, I have come for you."

He knew as he asked the question what its answer would be. "And what do you want of me?"

"You received a letter from us telling you it was time to do your duty for Germany. You have enjoyed the fruits of being a German citizen. You live in this wonderful home on this lovely farm thanks to the graciousness of the Reich, and now it's time for you to repay that debt. You are needed in the army."

"In what capacity?"

"You're needed as a soldier in the east. It's time to stem the advance of the communist mongrels and to protect German families, including those such as yours here in Czechoslovakia. Every able-bodied man is needed for the cause. Surely a man such as you, a German man with a wife and three children and with all that has been given you, surely such a man is ready to do his part and make sure his loved ones don't live as pigs." The man stubbed out his cigarette as he finished.

"But haven't I been of service to you already? Hasn't the German cause benefitted from the produce of this farm under my watch?"

"It has, and it's appreciated, but it's been no more than you should do. Now it's time for you to do more. I'm sure the other people here can take care of things in your absence."

Herman stalled for a moment, trying to find an argument that would let him stay with his family. "Is there no one to whom I can appeal this?"

"Appeal this?" There was a sardonic laugh from the man. "If you are a believer, it might be good to appeal to God for your safe return after a glorious victory for the Fatherland and the Führer."

"But . . ."

"No! There will be no further discussion."

"And when does my service start?" He knew the answer already; the letter and the man's behavior had made it clear.

"You will leave with me today."

"Do you know my destination?"

"Were you not listening earlier? You're headed east."

"May I ask what training I will receive before being sent to the front?"

"You're a man and a farmer. You'll do fine. Only city boys need training. You know how to shoot a gun, I'm sure."

"Yes, of course."

"And you know how to keep your wits about you. There! Your training is completed."

Herman fought the urge to strike the rude ugly man standing in his house, who was treating him as one would mistreat a servant. "If you will excuse me. I need to go talk with my wife."

"You're excused, but meet me here in this room in no more than an hour, and you won't need to bring anything. We will have your weapon and your uniform."

An hour later, Herman was walking down the steps with the man, leaving his devastated wife and son on the porch. The Czech men, realizing something was wrong when Herman hadn't returned to the field, had come to the house and were standing on the hill taking in the scene with their wives alongside. They watched as Herman got in the sidecar and left with the man, and they knew chances were it would be a long time before they saw him again, if they ever did. The distance that had grown between the Czech and German families disappeared as they watched Herman taken away, while his wife, with Elsa on one side and Georg on the other, stood at the top of the steps and watched him leave. After the motorcycle passed through the farm's heavy gate, the women went to comfort Johanna while the men stood by, shifting their weight from one foot to the other and saying nothing.

That night, Johanna lay awake and thought about her husband, sitting on a train with others like him, headed east, with every kilometer taking him farther away and closer to an unspeakable nightmare. Hours later, she lay there still trying to quiet her mind when Georg came into her room, sniffling and telling her he couldn't sleep. She patted the bed, letting him know it would be okay for him to sleep in her bed that night, while wondering if Herman would ever sleep next to her again.

Georg refused to go to school the next day, and Johanna didn't force him. She had a thousand things to think about, and she knew he wouldn't learn much that day. She sat at the breakfast table with him, feeling sorry for the two of them; then she pictured Herman and knew his morning must be a thousand times worse. Knowing he'd want her to be strong, and remembering he was sure she could do it, she chose to put her energy into the house and farm. She vowed that when Herman returned everything would be as good as it was when he left.

Detlef and Elsa joined them in the kitchen, saying a quiet good morning as they did. Elsa poured two cups of coffee while Detlef took a seat next to Johanna. When Elsa handed him his coffee, he took a sip, set his cup down, and said, "I will make sure things go well on this farm. You can trust me on that."

It was all Johanna could do not to laugh at him. Detlef, safe from the conflict thanks to his injuries. Detlef, the man who seemed to create more problems than he solved. It was this Detlef sitting here safe in her kitchen and sipping his coffee who was going to be the man to take charge while Herman was gone!

She gathered herself. "Thank you for that, Detlef. When we finish breakfast, I want you to go fetch Filip and bring him to the sitting room. We need to review Herman's instructions."

"I can do that."

"Good."

She set down her coffee cup. "Would you like some more bread, Georg?" The boy nodded yes, and she got up to fix it for him. She let Elsa take care of herself and Detlef.

Within the hour, Filip had come to meet with Johanna and Detlef. Johanna began the discussion. "So here we are, where none of us wanted to be, but let's give credit to Herman, we have a plan."

Filip said, "We do, but I'm sorry the time has come for it."

She showed a thin smile. "Thank you for that. We hoped and prayed this day would never come, but it has, and it's up to us to make sure the farm keeps running as it has been. Who knows? By God's grace, Herman may be back by autumn, and we want him to be pleased with what he sees when that day comes."

Filip fidgeted for moment, then said, "I'm sure he'll be back, if not by fall, then soon after. Herman's a smart man, and he'll do everything he can to get home to you, to your children, and to this farm."

She smiled again, still thin and forced. She was on the verge of tears, but somehow, she managed to smile.

Filip continued, "And know that you have the support of the families here. We'll do more than we've ever done to help you. This is our home, too, and we have every interest in its doing just as well—dare I say better than before."

Detlef said, "The family would expect nothing less of you."

Johanna shot him a glance, then faced Filip again. "We know the plan is a good one, Filip, and you are the one to make sure it's carried out. For the time being, humor me and come by each day to report on how things are going. Eventually I am sure fewer meetings will be needed."

Filip looked at Detlef, who sat there without speaking, his eyes going from Filip to Johanna and back again. "And I'm sure Detlef will prove to be a great help to me." It complimented Detlef while cementing Filip's place as the lead man, and Detlef had no choice but to agree.

Johanna smiled at Filip's tactic. "Okay then, let's discuss what will happen in the coming weeks. Are we set for the summer girls to return?"

"We are."

"And is all going well with the planting?"

"We're a bit behind, but we'll catch up."

"And so, what do you need from me today, Filip?"

"Just what we have done this morning. Detlef and I will go meet with the others. Letting them know that things will move ahead as if Herman were here will be welcome news, I think."

Detlef looked to Johanna, wondering if she'd prefer to go with Filip instead, but she signaled her agreement that he be the one. "Detlef, you can tell me how the meeting goes."

When they'd left the house and made it down the steps, Filip turned and walked purposefully to the field to find the men, with Detlef shuffling along behind him. Filip stopped to allow a breathless Detlef to catch up, and then they stood side by side as they met the men. Filip reminded Jan and Marek how things would be. His speech was short and precise and its message clear. Detlef stood at his side, quiet for once, nodding at Filip's words.

❧ 19 ❧

The Children Return from School

Summer 1944

Johanna, Elsa, and Olexa went to Prague in May to bring their daughters and Rolf home for the summer. Annelise and Rolf hadn't been told about their father yet, because that wasn't the kind of news a mother puts in a letter. When the women made it to the girls' room, Rolf was there waiting, the four of them talking excitedly the way students do when breaks from school are about to begin.

Seeing them so excited made Johanna's task all the more difficult. She'd rehearsed what she would say repeatedly on the train, but now that she was in the room she didn't know where to start. As it turned out, her children could tell from her expression something was wrong.

Annelise rose and went to Johanna. "Mother, what is it? You don't seem happy to see us."

"Oh, Annelise, it isn't that. I have some difficult news to share. Several weeks ago, your father was drafted into service and sent to the Russian Front."

Annelise put her hand to her face in shock, so it was up to Rolf to ask the next question. "Is he . . . is he okay?"

"Yes, he is as of his last letter, and he wanted to make sure that you knew he was doing well, and that he'd be with us again someday."

Tears came to Annelise, and her mother hugged her, but Rolf reacted in a different way, yelling out in anger and punching the wall in the girls' room so hard he hurt his fist. He then ripped off the shirt of the Hitler Youth and put it in his bag. Wearing a uniform had appealed to him at first, but after hearing of his father, he hated it, and he'd never wear it again. Within minutes, he channeled his anger into determination, and he let his mother know he had no intention of returning to school when fall came. Instead he would stay and help her on the farm.

Johanna didn't argue, thinking he'd change his mind by fall. She calmed him down and helped him find another shirt to wear for the journey home, secretly glad he'd removed the other. Although she knew he'd joined the group because of pressure from the other boys, she still detested that shirt and everything about the regime that had taken Herman from them.

Not long after they made it back to Strednitz, eight summer girls arrived, and the one who'd caused trouble the previous summer was one of them. She was a different person, no longer the silly girl of June nor the one who hardly said a word after returning from her temporary banishment. She was happy now, she worked as hard as any, and she had become something of a leader who was well-liked by all the girls. One of the others happened to mention the change they saw, and she whispered she'd fallen in love with a boy in the village and hoped to marry him before the next summer. She had no time for foolishness now.

Rolf had grown during the past year, and he threw himself into work on the farm, attempting to fill the void left by his father's absence. He was impatient with Georg and ordered him to be quicker with his lessons so that he could get to the field earlier to help. Georg didn't mind. He hated spelling as much as ever, and he was happy to go to the fields. Annelise was happy as well, because there were other things that needed her attention. After working with Georg on his spelling each day, she'd head to the field to join the others or stay in the house and help her mother in the kitchen. Johanna was proud of Annelise and Rolf, thinking they seemed more like adults than children, but along with the pride she felt some regret that their youth was essentially gone.

They didn't know Herman's exact location. The only return address he gave them was a five-digit code used by the German mail service to identify troop locations. His letters were infrequent, at best. When he did write, he told them he was among good men, both young and old, and the more experienced men were helpful to the new ones, showing them how to be brave but not so bold they put themselves in more danger than they already faced.

Herman wrote that he was proud to be protecting those in Czechoslovakia from the Russians. Proud was never a word Herman used, so Johanna suspected it was his way of showing patriotism without lavishing praise on the Nazis, and that he did so with an eye to making sure his letters made it through.

He begged for news of the farm, and Johanna wrote often. He would respond to her news, letting her know he'd read her mail. She was overjoyed each time a letter arrived, because that meant he was alive, at least on the day of its writing. Of course something terrible could have happened since that day, and she tried not to think of that, but eventually worry would return, staying until his next letter came. When it did, the cycle of relief and worry would begin again.

———

Sometime in June there came a different tide of people, this one headed in the opposite direction of the soldiers. Wagon after wagon of German families were headed west, fleeing the Russian advance. Some would stop at the farm, and Johanna would invite them inside for a meal and a moment of rest before moving on. They sat at her table, enjoying a break from the difficult life on the road and telling her their stories.

They told her that before they took to the road, they'd heard fighting in the distance, and soon those sounds were growing closer, so there came a day they had no choice but to gather up what they could and take flight. It was a difficult decision, but they knew if they'd stayed, they would have faced almost certain death. Travel was difficult, and some of the refugees shared stories of troubles along the way. The Czech Partisans, emboldened by the weakening German position, had increased their attacks, and Germans in wagons were easy targets for them.

"Travel together when the time comes," more than one traveler told them. The message wasn't lost on them.

The letters from Herman stopped coming, and not hearing from him worried Johanna. The days went by, and it was impossible for her to hide her concern from her children. They'd look to her for reassurance, and she'd say, "We'll hear tomorrow, I'm sure of it." Finally after three weeks, a letter arrived. While the mail always showed wear and tear, this one showed more, so most likely several officials had looked at it. Still, it was a letter from Herman, and after three weeks it was one of the most beautiful things Johanna had ever seen.

She tore the letter open and saw her name scrawled at the top. Herman had nearly perfect penmanship, but his letters were hurried and messy. What more could be expected from men on the Russian Front with little time allowed for writing? He began the letter by responding to the farm and family news Johanna had shared in her last letter. She could feel the longing in his words as she read his reply. Then came a part of the letter that sounded very different.

> I have been thinking. When fall comes and the crops have been harvested, why don't you pack up the wagon and take the children to see Peter? I know the children will be in school then, but they should be excused for such an excursion. Load the wagon with produce from the fields. I know Peter and his wife will enjoy eating something better than what they now have. You should probably take blankets and clothing for cold weather, since it is so unpredictable in fall.
>
> I'm sure the families on the farm can look after things while you're away. Filip will make sure everything is taken care of until your return. Who knows? Maybe we will have won this war by then, and I can join you in Frankfurt and return with you to our farm.
>
> Think about it please. You might want to consider going through Bavaria. It's lovely in the fall. I'm sure Detlef, Elsa, and Emma would enjoy the trip as well, and company on the road might be a good thing.
>
> All my love,
> Your Herman

Later in the evening she read the last part of the letter to Elsa, then put it on the table and looked at her sister. Elsa dried the last dish, then sat across from her sister. "Why would he want us to plan a trip to see Peter?"

Johanna made a little noise as she pursed her lips and exhaled. "I think he was hiding a message in there. If he'd come out and said the war is being lost and it's time for us to flee, then maybe his letter wouldn't make it past the officials who check every piece of mail. It's obvious his letter has been read, so it appears he chose his words well. Elsa, I think he's telling us we should consider leaving here and going to safety in Germany."

"I see. Well, it isn't as if we haven't thought about leaving."

"No. But he doesn't know that for sure. Maybe he thinks I'm not planning to leave until he comes home."

"That could be."

"So tell me, what do you think?"

Elsa thought about it before speaking. "Well, it seems to me, waiting and hoping for the German army to turn the tide is not a good plan. It may not happen—probably won't happen now—and we should plan accordingly for our own safety." She paused, then gazed blankly into the distance as if she couldn't believe what she was about to say. "So leaving is the only option."

Johanna brushed a wisp of hair from her forehead. "So many of those who have stopped here had no destination in mind other than getting to safety somewhere in Germany, and I've wondered what kind of life they will have when they arrive. And then I think, what kind of life will we have? It'll be nothing like we've had here in Strednitz." Johanna paused and looked at her sister. "And I want to stay here to make sure Herman is able to reunite with us, so I'm conflicted."

Elsa walked to stand by her sister and put her arms around her. "His letter tells you that you need to take care of yourself and your children, and if that means leaving here, then we leave."

"But to Frankfurt? That might be a difficult journey."

"Maybe he just mentioned it to get you to think about going. Maybe going to Frankfurt just means for you to go to Germany and find somewhere safe to wait. You know that he won't rest until he finds you."

"I suppose you're right."

"This time I know I am, Johanna."

So with grim determination the two families stayed on, all the while knowing their day to leave Strednitz was coming. Not long after Herman's letter, Herr Ritter came, bringing Günter Pöhlmann with him. The two men met with Johanna, Detlef, and Elsa and talked about their situation. After some discussion, they agreed to stay as long as they could, but when the time came to leave, the families needed to be ready. They would travel together with other German families in Strednitz and Vysoka and hope to meet up with others from Melník somewhere along the way. Maybe their friends the Ritters would be among them.

The three Czech families were interested bystanders during all this. They had witnessed the German refugees coming through, and they knew what that might mean for the two German families in the big house. Katerina had overheard the meeting with Ritter and Pöhlmann, and she shared what she'd heard with Filip. They knew that the Germans might soon need to leave the farm. They also knew that when Johanna and her family chose to leave, it would change things on the farm. While the Czechs were eager to see their country free of the puppet regime of Emil Hácha, and the hated Nazis expelled, and they looked forward to a day only Czech families lived on the estate, there were mixed feelings about seeing the two families go. They had been treated fairly by them, and the farm had done well, and while they felt the farm rightfully belonged to them, questions remained as to how it would be when Johanna and the others were gone. Filip had been lead assistant under the German families. Would he take over when they were gone? And how would things be sorted out among the others? And beyond that, what would life be like in Bohemia—in Czechoslovakia at large—after the war? Who would govern the country? Would the Big Bear to the east leave them alone when its army had made its way through their homeland, or would the Americans beat the Russians to it, and what kind of future would that hold?

As summer wound down, word reached the farm that Prague was being bombed, making it unsafe for the older children to return to school, so they stayed on the farm. It was yet another sign the situation was worsening; the time to leave was coming.

When the eight girls left in late August, there were promises they'd all return the next summer, but as she heard those promises, Johanna knew her family wouldn't be living there when that time came. It had always been somewhat sad when summer ended and the girls left, but this time it was a heavier, more overwhelming feeling, approaching grief. Young women from the villages had come to the farm during the summers of 1942, '43, and '44, and they'd filled those three summers with activity and productivity. Maybe the girls would return in 1945, but if they did, they would be helping Filip and the others.

The next evening, Johanna, along with Elsa and Detlef, began to make more definite plans for their departure. Rolf joined in, as did Annelise. He took part in the discussions, while Annelise chose to listen. With Herman away, Rolf had tried to be the man of the family, and he felt he should be involved in the planning. He didn't speak much, but when he did he had good input. Johanna reminded them of Herman's recommendations that they wait until the harvest was completed, which would provide the travelers with food for their journey west and allow for those who stayed to be provisioned as well. They agreed that would be the best scenario if time and the tides of war allowed.

No one else spoke for a moment. Finally, Elsa broke the silence. "It is just as Herman told us in his letter, so I think it's the right thing to do."

Johanna agreed, then said, "I'll let Filip know when he and I meet tomorrow."

Heads nodded, and it was silent again. There was so much to consider: sadness at the thought of saying farewell to life in Strednitz, preoccupation with plans to be made, worries about what the trip might have in store, and as always, thoughts of Herman.

———

"So that's our plan, Filip. We'll stay through the harvest unless things take a turn for the worse and we must leave sooner. And then it will be yours, this wonderful farm. Yours and the other families. And I think you'll do well with it."

Filip sat in Herman's office with Johanna. He smiled, but it was a guarded one. "Johanna, you and Herman have been wonderful caretakers of the farm, but I won't lie, it's a day we've looked forward to, the day when it is a Czech farm once again. Still, we will worry for you and your family when you take to the road. It will be so full of trouble for you."

"It could well be, but there might be trouble here as well."

"So long as forces outside our control leave us alone, we'll be okay."

"What are those forces, Filip?"

He looked at his hand and then used his fingers to make his point. "I see three dangers to the farm at least—one from the Germans as they retreat, followed by a threat from the advancing army, the Russians or Americans, whoever that may be, and then there could be a third threat from our own countrymen, the Partisans."

Johanna listened intently. Most of her time had been spent planning for the departure, so Filip's words had her attention. "Those three dangers you speak of, have you given thought as to how you might prepare for them?"

Her question impressed Filip. It was exactly what should be asked. "We have. We know if the soldiers come . . . when they come, they'll be looking for food, and a farm like this will be a prime target for them. We know that soldiers are ill-fed, and they'll be hungry. Our animals will be tempting, and I'm sure they won't last long, and the soldiers will most likely take what's stored in the pantries and cellars, leaving little for us there."

"You could never stop that from happening, Filip. To resist would put you and the others in danger. Is there a way to save some provisions from their thievery?"

"Yes, we've already identified places to hide food where they will never look. We'll hide it as we harvest and pray for the winter's snow to provide additional cover. We should have enough to make it if all other food is taken. But we'll have to ration it, I'm sure. And one other thing—we'll tell the soldiers that the German families took much of the food with them and left us very little. This may help us when the Partisans come around, and it might help separate us from any association with the Germans who lived here."

"I see. And you'll plant more winter grains this year, I suppose?"

Again, her question impressed him. "Yes, and a bigger crop should help us get through. Even if we're looted over winter, the spring grains will ensure we'll have bread if nothing else. We won't starve. And again, all of this is the worst possible case. Maybe we'll be bypassed. Strednitz isn't on a main route; there's no train station. We won't be a military objective. And with the grace of God, we'll be circumvented by the fighting."

"So then, Filip, we are left to hope for good weather for the coming harvest, so that all our plans will be easily carried out."

"Yes. If ever there was a time for good weather and an early harvest, this would be it."

Johanna had so many other things she wanted to say that day, but a better day to say them might be coming, and maybe she'd have just the right words when it did.

❦ 20 ❧

Three Worlds

Autumn 1944

Soon, German soldiers appeared in Vysoka, and Georg would pedal into town to speak with them. On one of those days, he watched them cutting trees and piling them by the road that led into town from the east.

When one of the soldiers stopped his work for a moment, Georg asked, "Why are you cutting our trees?"

The man answered, "Maybe you are a Russian spy, and we shouldn't tell you." His partners laughed at his teasing.

"I'm Georg Mueller. My father fights for Germany, and I'm not a spy."

"How old are you?"

"I am eight. I'll be nine when spring comes."

The soldier with the smile looked at his partners and said, "Shall we trust this one?"

His partners grinned and nodded, glad to take a break from their work to talk to the boy.

The man continued, "We're cutting the trees and stacking them by the main road. If the Russians come, we'll pile the trees across the road and block their way."

"Oh." Georg thought about it for another moment, then asked, "But won't they have tanks, and can't they just go around the town?"

"You should be a general with such insight. Yes, but if they do, it may save the town, and it will take them longer with no road to use. Every delay helps. Maybe they'll reach a point where they'll stop, content with their position, and the fighting will come to an end, but more likely the delays will give Germany time to find something new to use to turn the tide of battle, and then all the villages will be safe again."

One of the others said, "Or maybe we are just following foolish orders from ignorant men."

"Josef!"

"I've said what I've said. No one heard it but us and the boy." He bent down and looked Georg in the eye. "Will you tell anyone, my little general?"

"No. But I might tell someone that you're cutting our trees."

"I think we can allow that. Along with you now. We need to get back to work."

Seeing that the men weren't going to pay any more attention to him, Georg got back on his bike and headed home.

A few days later, a soldier came to the Muellers' home to advise them that it would soon be necessary for them to leave the farm and make their way to Germany, and he'd come back when it was time. Herr Pöhlmann stopped by the next day, and they revisited their plans to leave. When he left, Johanna walked through the rooms of the house at Strednitz. While it was never home the way Tariverde was, it had been better than anything since then, and likely better than anything they'd have again.

She thought of the day they met the families and how awkward it had been at first. She thought of Christmases and summers and all the good times there had been. She had known it was a situation that wouldn't last forever, but with the end of it looming now, she wanted to bargain for more time. It was going to be hard to say goodbye, and whatever came after that would be difficult at best, and full of peril at worst.

She thought of her three children and wanted nothing more than for them to be safe and have some kind of future when the war was finally over. She wanted Herman with her to help make that happen, but until he returned, it was her job, and she had to do it well.

Unlike their leaving Tariverde, there would be no one to organize their departure and no one to set a destination for them. They'd be relying on their own wits and those of the others who'd travel with them. And then there was Herman. How would he know where they were? What would they do to survive until he found them?

They lived in three worlds that autumn. There was the day-to-day world of the farm, which was the best of the three. Ordinary chores and challenges were both a distraction and a comfort, and the family threw themselves into every task.

The second world revolved around preparing for their escape to

Germany—a world in which Rolf and Annelise proved to be a great help, as was Aunt Elsa and their cousin Emma. On the other hand, Detlef had reinjured his back one day working alone in a stall with a calf, and while it didn't cripple him, the pain rendered him unable to perform physical labor. He withdrew inside himself and was little help, even in the planning.

The third world was one of worry for Herman. As fall turned toward winter, it had been six months since he'd been taken from them. They were encouraged that they'd gotten no bad news and hoped that meant he'd been spared from harm, but all along the three-thousand-kilometer front, every man was in harm's way. Bullets, grenades, artillery fire, aerial attacks, and tank assaults put men in danger, and there were no safe zones.

Sometime during that summer and fall, two more of Peter's sons had lost their lives, one along that same Eastern Front and the other in a battle somewhere near Sevastopol. The only one still alive was the youngest, who was serving in the most dangerous of the branches, the Luftwaffe. Communication didn't reach people as it had earlier, so some time elapsed before news of their sons' deaths reached Peter and his wife. Their neighborhood in Frankfurt had been bombed by the Allies, and much of the city was reduced to rubble. Thousands died in the bombing, including men with whom Peter worked and some of their neighbors. Food was scarce, and fuel for heating even more so. And they, too, worried for Herman. There couldn't have been a bleaker time for the family of Peter Mueller.

On the night the first snow fell in central Bohemia, Johanna sat at the table with the rest of the family. "The harvest is done, and I think we have all the food ready for our trip. We'll only need to load it into our wagons, along with the other necessities we'll take with us, and we can be on our way."

Detlef asked, "How shall we decide what to leave and what to take? Perhaps one's necessity is another's luxury."

Johanna tried not to show her impatience. The topic had been discussed for weeks now, but Detlef hadn't been an active participant. She looked at him and said, "Detlef, we've discussed this."

"I know, but I wouldn't mind going over it again if that would suit you."

"Sure. A little review might be helpful to us all. So Detlef, why don't you tell me what you would consider a necessity."

"Blankets, I think. Yes, we'll need blankets for the cold."

"Those for sure. And what else?"

Detlef had his next answer ready. "Well, winter clothing, if we leave in winter, which it now appears we will. You have the food organized, you said?"

"Yes, we have that."

"Okay. We'll need firewood for warmth and cooking."

"Do you think it would be better to take that or gather it along the way?"

Detlef hesitated, considering his answer. Elsa and the children were patient, allowing him time. They knew most of this had been gone through several times, but they forgave him. He was in pain most of the time.

"I think we take a little wood, but we gather most of it. That will leave room in our wagons for other things."

"Yes, but as you say, we'll take a little. Maybe enough for a fire or two. After all, you will have three people in your wagon and we'll have four in ours, so there won't be much room for things, and food should be a priority. We have the journey to Germany, which should take a few weeks, and then we will want some food even there with things being so uncertain. Clothing and blankets come next. Basic tools such as an axe and shovel, basic household items such as pots and pans and utensils to use for eating are next, and maybe there'll be room for a couple of our most prized possessions, but there won't be room for more than that."

"And water, we'll have to find that along the way."

"Yes."

"And for our horses? They'll need to eat too."

"We'll need to take some grain for them. It's winter. We don't know what we'll find for grazing."

Detlef sighed. "We'll need more than two wagons for all of this."

"Two wagons are all we have."

In the quiet that followed, Annelise had a different question. "What happens to the Czech families once we leave, Mother?"

Johanna smiled, impressed at how grown-up her daughter had become. "It's a question the Czech families will have to resolve."

———————

At that same moment at a point along the Eastern Front, two soldiers were talking—one young, and one old enough to be his father. The younger man had just asked if the war had already been lost.

Herman considered his young companion's question. "I think it might be. We're defending German soil now."

The young man looked at Herman. "If the front has moved this far west, then that might mean the Russians will be near your home in Strednitz."

"It might."

"I hope your family is safe, Herman."

"My Johanna will know to leave before the war reaches them. If they haven't already left, they're organized and ready. I suggested it to her in a letter. I know she understood my meaning and she's already done what she needs to do."

"You think so?"

"I'm sure of it."

The young man paused as he tried to picture the family Herman had described to him. He imagined them busily loading wagons with their belongings and preparing to flee the advancing Russian army.

"It would be so difficult to consider what to take and what to leave, I'd imagine."

Herman took in a breath and exhaled. "We've done this before. They'll know."

"Oh, that's right. You have—and more than once you've told me. I'm sorry."

"It's okay. It simply means that my wife, her sister, and her brother-in-law have experience with these things. They'll get the food organized and pack only the necessities for the trip. She'll take a few personal things but not many—the Bible for sure."

The boy sniffed. "The Bible! A lot of good that's done us! There are prayers all over Germany for us, yet the war is lost."

Herman was thoughtful for a moment. "Prayer doesn't work in times like these, because there is no place for God in war. God is found in peace, and he takes no sides in politics or war. He didn't create us to kill each other, to destroy the land, to bring misery such as this to the world. He'll return to this world someday, but only when we've come to our senses."

"Do you think you and I will make it home when that time has come?"

Herman had his doubts. Who wouldn't, with the two of them there along the front with men dying around them every day? He wanted the young man to have hope, so he said, "I think we will. I've a family to get home to, and you'll have a son or daughter by then."

The young man smiled as he thought of his young wife and the baby she was carrying. "Yes. Sometimes I feel bad that I put my bride in that situation. Just married! And then we learned of the pregnancy just before I left." He paused. "I'm not sure what I was thinking."

Herman chuckled quietly, because no one ever laughed out loud with the enemy lurking. "Thinking seldom has anything to do with babies. If it did, there wouldn't be as many of them."

The young man laughed, quickly covering his mouth. "That's true, although if I can be honest, I wanted her to get pregnant."

"You did?"

"Yes, I wanted something left of me in the world if I didn't make it home."

Herman looked back at the boy, eighteen at most and looking even younger. "I understand that. To be honest, I've had that same thought about my three, but when I think it, then I'm only more determined to make it home."

The young soldier sighed. "I hope we have a son."

"I hope so, too, but I love my Annelise as much as the boys. Some days more." He got a big smile. "Boys can be a handful."

"But they carry on our family name."

Herman exclaimed, "Ahhh! That's overrated I believe. I think you'll have your boy. If not this one, then the next one, for sure." Herman knew there was no guarantee to anything he'd said, but it had been a horrendous twenty-four hours, and he could feel the boy's discouragement. He hoped the thought of a son would give his protégé hope. If the boy lost hope, he might have no reason to use caution, and men lacking that didn't last long on the Eastern Front.

21

Christmastime

December 1944

Johanna was faced with her first Christmas without Herman, so she decided to make a bleak time as joyous as possible for her children. She sent out invitations to the other families to join hers for Christmas dinner. She and Elsa, along with Annelise and Emma, spent the days leading up to Christmas filling the kitchen with the tempting aromas of favorite Christmas dishes.

The boys weren't expected to help in the kitchen. Still, that didn't prevent them from being underfoot, so Johanna sent them out to gather greenery for decorations. It would keep them busy and add to the festivity. All too soon they returned with armfuls of wild juniper, and they were in the way again, so she sent them to the two rooms where dinner would be served and told them to arrange the greenery. It was afternoon by then, so she reminded them to pull the blackout shades before sundown. She wanted the rooms to be bright and cheerful that night, and the shades that had been installed after the planes started flying overhead were the only way the lights could be on.

The boys made short work of arranging greenery and pulling the shades, and they were soon back in the kitchen, underfoot again, and looking for any treat they could find. Johanna finally relented and gave them each some lebkuchen. Seeing them enjoy the treat took her back to their first Christmas on the farm, and she smiled as she remembered her Herman pestering her almost as much as the boys.

They had their eyes on another cookie when Johanna assigned them the task of setting the big table in the dining room, as well as the two small tables in the sitting room for the children. She knew it was a risky request. Her boys were never the most careful, and the tables would be set haphazardly at best, but it was something for them to do, and their disorder could easily be made right.

In their home near the big house, Mrs. Novák and her daughters were preparing some traditional Czech dishes to go along with the German fare that Johanna and the others were fixing. In the Dvorák home, Jan had fallen asleep while Teresa worked on mending. Their children were playing a game of checkers on a well-worn board Jan had been given as a boy.

In the next house beyond the Dvoráks', Marek and Veronica were trying to be quiet while the children were asleep, but they were whispering excitedly about the news they planned to share at dinner.

By half past five o'clock, the food was ready, the chores completed on the farm, and all the families gathered in the dining room. Johanna looked around at the twenty-one faces crowded around her and at a table loaded with food and decorated with greenery, and everything looked perfect under the glow of the chandelier. The room was full of life, lacking only Herman, whose presence would have made it perfect.

Annelise delivered a prayer in German, then repeated it in Czech. The Czechs were moved by her doing so, and there were smiles and tears at her thoughtfulness.

Johanna told everyone to take a seat. The Novák family sat across from the Dvoráks, and the Muellers at the head of the table with the four Czernýs. Zuzana, the eldest Novák daughter, had married during the fall, so she and her young husband were added to the adults at the dining room table. The children were seated at tables in the sitting room, with the girls sitting at the larger table and the boys at the smaller one.

They'd barely started eating when Marek Czerný pushed his chair back, stood up, and proudly announced that a third Czerný child was due in the late spring. While his words were Czech, it was clear even to the Germans what he was saying. Everyone applauded and looked at Veronica, who quietly but matter-of-factly had Filip tell them that this would be their last, then stared at Marek to make sure the message was received. Marek gave his wife the look of a boy who'd been reprimanded, then broke into a broad smile. He turned to Filip and said, "Yes, I think three will be sufficient," then gave his wife a kiss on the cheek. After Filip's translation, Johanna wished the Czernýs well, all the while thinking she would never get to see that baby.

With the future so uncertain, it was better that the mealtime conversation focus on favorite Christmas memories, with the Nováks busily translating each story as it was told. The room was alive with noisy conversation and laughter, and the evening passed all too quickly.

Then, as they were enjoying their desserts, Johanna felt it was time to address something that had been on her mind. "So, Filip, I know you and the others have had conversations about what lies ahead for you. Would you consider it rude if I asked how those conversations have gone?"

Filip gestured to all the people seated at the table. "First of all, I want to say what a credit it is to you that you're worried about what will become of us after you leave. I think very few people would have that concern when faced with their own uncertainties. And yes, we've planned, and yes again, I'd be happy to share those plans with you."

Johanna knew what she was about to hear might be difficult. It would drive home that her family's time at #1 Strednitz was near its end. Still, the farm had been good to her family for three years, and she wanted the best for it and for the families gathered with her that evening. "Yes, if you'd care to share them, I'd like to know."

Before he began, he took a moment to speak to the others and tell them what was happening. Little Anna Czerný was getting restless, so she was sent to the room with the children. The only other child who needed to be attended to was Georg, who'd annoyed the girls to the extent they came in and complained about him. Johanna called Georg in and asked him if he'd prefer to stay with the others or spend the evening in his room. He thought staying with the others would be a better choice, so his mother let him know what was expected of him if he wished to stay. That dealt with, the table grew quiet, and the others looked from Johanna to Filip as he spoke.

"We think it would be good for there to be four Czech families here, with one in each of the four houses. While that might not protect the farm against German soldiers coming through or the Russians or Americans who may come next, it would at least provide some security against marauding Partisans. They could be our biggest concern, but they'll be less likely to harass us or steal from us if they see Czechs in each home."

"I see, and who will be living here in this house? Please tell me it will be you and Katerina."

"Yes, that's been agreed to, and I will continue to direct the activities of the farm."

"And in your house? Will it be Jan and Teresa?"

He looked at the Dvoráks. "Surprisingly, no. They've chosen to remain in their home. Jan will take my position as the lead assistant, the person in charge if I'm not around, but he has no interest in moving." When Jan heard his name, he knew what was being discussed. He smiled and nodded.

"So, who then? Marek?"

Filip gestured toward Marek and Veronica. "Yes, the Czernýs will be moving to our current home." Then, laughing, he said, "And with this evening's news, it seems they could use the space."

Johanna looked at Zuzana Novák and her young husband. "I think I know the fourth family. Let me see if I'm correct."

"If you guessed these two, then you've guessed correctly."

"That's wonderful, Filip! I couldn't be happier with this arrangement, and we'll leave here knowing the farm will be in good hands."

Filip stood and said first in Czech, then in German, "We will pray for your safety when you leave."

Johanna gestured toward the families gathered around her. "And I will pray for all of you."

When her husband's translation was completed, Katerina scoffed, "So many prayers are being sent to God, who can be sure He listens to them all?"

Filip put his arm around his wife's shoulder. "We'll do our best as we wait for ours to reach His ears."

Only the Czechs understood the exchange, but the patience in Filip's voice was unmistakable.

The seriousness of the discussion dampened the mood, and Johanna had some regrets that she'd chosen that night to discuss it. The mood improved, but it was never quite as happy as it had been earlier. When Johanna spoke about it later with her sister, Elsa told her not to blame herself. The evening was inevitably going to end with some melancholy in the air. Things hadn't been the same for a while, and they would only change more in the next few weeks. Everyone understood that.

As the evening wound down, the guests rose to leave, thanking Johanna for her hospitality. She walked them to the door and wished them all a Happy Christmas. The Nováks stayed so that Katerina could gather up her dishes. As Johanna waited for her to do that, she knew there would be just one more noteworthy conversation with the other families, and that would be on the day it was time for her family to leave. There was something she wanted to say before then. "Filip, I want to thank the two of you for being so good to work with, for being so welcoming to a family you didn't have to welcome, for working to keep peace on the farm and keeping everyone committed to its success when there easily could have been friction, and for making this farm better each year under your care. Maybe there'll be a day that the world will be right again, and Herman and I can come back to visit you."

"The door will be open when you do."

They stood, and for the first time in the three years that Johanna had been on the farm, she hugged Filip Novák and his wife. Things were difficult before the Mueller family came to Strednitz, but looking back on their time there, particularly that part of it before Herman was taken away, it seemed almost idyllic. How long before life would be good again? Would it ever be?

❦ 22 ❧

The End Approaches

Winter 1945

As 1944 became 1945, the tide of refugees continued through the village. They usually traveled in groups, but there was one family who came through alone. They stopped in front of the house for a time as if considering what to do, then entered the property through the open gate. When they got to the base of the steps, the man got off the wagon and slowly made his way up the hill, his hat in hand. Johanna and the children came out on the porch to see what he wanted, and he fidgeted nervously with his hat, then asked in German if they might stay overnight. Johanna looked at the man standing there, cold and discouraged, with his wife and children down the hill, huddled under blankets in the wagon. "Yes, please come join us." She turned to her children standing beside her. "Rolf, you and Georg help the man with his horses." Then turning back to the man, she said, "Tell your family to come in. Do you have anything you need brought in for the night for safekeeping?"

"A few things. We didn't bring much."

"Well, we'll help with that too."

The team was unhitched, and Rolf and Georg took them to the stable and gave them some food. Of course their animals wanted food as well, so they took care of them. The family unloaded what needed to be brought inside for the night with the help of Annelise and Emma. Johanna had them put their things in the mudroom. When the boys got back from the barn, she had them show the family to their bedroom. The boys would sleep on the floor in the sitting room that night.

Later that evening as they sat at the dinner table, the man said, "It's so kind of you to share your home and this wonderful meal tonight."

"I'm sure you'd do the same if our situations were reversed."

"We would, and in fact we did for a few who came through our village before it was our time to leave."

"May I ask why you're traveling alone?"

"We left before the rest of our party. I was ready to go, and we heard the fighting getting closer. I am sure the rest will catch us soon, or we'll join others."

Detlef looked across a table that was full for the first time since Christmas, and he asked, "How many days have you been on the road?"

"Just a few." He looked at Detlef, then at Johanna, and knew his answer had hit home. After a moment, he continued, "I'm so sorry, but I think you too will have to leave soon. The fighting isn't far away now. You might have a month, but no more." He looked around the dining room. "Our home was nice, but not nearly so nice as this, and now we must go to Germany and hope we can find some situation there where we can have a home once again." He paused, then added, "And you'll be joining us soon and doing the same I think, and with nothing nearly so nice waiting for you."

It grew quiet because he spoke the truth. They would need to leave soon, and his concerns about what would await them were ones Johanna shared. Then remembering her role as hostess, Johanna said, "Then sleep well tonight, and if you don't want to leave tomorrow, stay another day and let the rest of your party catch up with you here at our house."

They did in fact spend another day at the farm, and the rest of their party caught up with them the second morning. As the refugee family waited for the others to arrive, the man begged Johanna to come with them. "You'll have to leave soon. Why not come with us now? You'll be leaving before the trouble gets too near and traveling with good people."

Johanna considered his offer, then thanked him and let him know she had an agreement with other families in the area, and her family wasn't leaving until they were ready to go. The refugees kept trying to convince her to come anyway, but Johanna politely declined. She wouldn't renege on the agreement, and even if there had been no agreement, she would have stayed. It wasn't time yet. It was coming she knew, but not on that day.

After their guests left, she and Rolf sat at the kitchen table reviewing plans one more time. Her Rolf was becoming more like his father every day, and while she loved that about him, it made her wish Herman could see how his oldest son had grown, and Annelise, as well.

✁ 23 ✍

Refugees

Winter 1945

By January, the Allies had entered Germany and were moving on Frankfurt. Zhukov and Konev had the Russians on German soil in the east, and there was speculation that an offensive would be launched from there as part of the campaign to take over Czechoslovakia. So it came as no surprise when, on a day in early February, soldiers came to their home and told Johanna the time had come to leave. Their news could have made her sad, but she was beyond that by then. She'd rehearsed the departure so many times, her mind moved instead to putting the plans they'd made into action.

On the day of their departure, the Muellers and Lehmanns spent the afternoon loading the wagons, and by nightfall they were loaded and ready. The three Czech families waited for the cover of darkness to come say goodbye. Partisan activity had been picking up, and for the Czech families to be seen displaying any sort of affection for the Germans might label them as collaborators and put them in danger of reprisals.

Farewells bring tears, even those that have long been expected, and the one on Strednitz farm that last night was no exception. The Czechs didn't stay long, knowing the two families would be getting up early in the morning to meet the rest of their group. Three years earlier, the Muellers had come to take over the farm from another German family. It wasn't a development the Czech families welcomed, but in time they learned that Herman and Johanna were fair and decent people. They heard of other families in similar situations who had to deal with arrogance and abuse. So, after three years of working side by side with each other, the gap between the Germans and Czechs on the farm had narrowed. While friendship might be too strong a word, it was as close as any other to describing their relationship, and that made the goodbye a protracted one, with repeated well-wishes from both sides. Finally, the Czechs left, but

Filip returned for the final farewell. "Johanna Mueller, we spoke not long ago about the dangers ahead for all of us, and we promised to pray for each other."

"Filip. I will pray for you and the rest we leave behind. You're a good man, and the others have also proven to be as good over our time here, and I only hope there's a time when prayers for good people are again answered, because it seems so long since they have been."

He nodded in agreement, appreciating her words, then quickly turned and left to join his wife and daughters on the porch. The Nováks had been the first family to greet the Muellers, and they were the last to say goodbye, which was as it should be.

The Muellers and Lehmanns finished cleaning up. Johanna wanted everything perfect for the Nováks when they moved in. It would never be perfect enough, but when she was satisfied they went to their beds for the final time. There was very little sleep that night for any of them, and sometime just before dawn, with Detlef's wagon leading the way and Rolf handling the reins in the Muellers' wagon, they rolled down the hill of #1 Strednitz and passed through the gates a final time.

They stopped in the road just outside the entrance, and Johanna directed Rolf to close the gates. As soon as he had done so and gotten back in their wagon, the Pöhlmanns and a few others from Strednitz and Vysoka joined them, and their party began its trek to Germany. They hoped to rendezvous with families coming out of Melník and Prague within the next few days, including, with any luck, the Ritters. The more wagons, the better, where safety was concerned.

As the sun got higher that first morning, Johanna thought of what must be happening back on the farm. Families would be moving that day, with three of the homes welcoming new occupants, including the newlyweds who'd be moving into the Czernýs' house. She smiled at that. The boy was barely nineteen, and a few years younger than his bride. Later that night, he and his bride would sleep in a bed in their own home, and it took her mind back to Tariverde and Herman.

She was especially happy for Zuzana. While she didn't know what it was, she had learned that Zuzana once had another young man in her life and that something had happened to end the relationship, breaking the girl's heart. She felt sure this young man would make a good husband.

It would have been so much better if they had motorized transportation, but they had none, and no fuel for it anyway. So it was an assemblage of slow-moving horse-drawn wagons making their way to German territory. If anything, the covered wagons resembled a line of prairie schooners headed across the great American west, but instead of the vastness of Nebraska and Wyoming, they were traveling through the fields and villages of southern Bohemia.

Having been warned that the Russians might be preparing an invasion that would come from Germany, they chose to go south rather than taking the shorter northwestern route. So a journey of eighty kilometers that would have taken a few days became a much longer one that would take them weeks, if not months.

With so many wagons, progress was slow. Even though they would rise at sunrise, it would take a while to get everyone ready to move, and as the end of the day approached, finding a place to camp was a priority. If an appropriate place was found mid-afternoon, they'd stop, choosing a location with room, water, and wood over traveling another kilometer or two.

The road was passable at first thanks to the ground being frozen, but as the days warmed, the snow melted, turning the road into a quagmire. Then came an unusually warm day with heavy rain, rendering the roads nearly impassable. Still they slogged on. The strain on the horses increased as time went by, and their fighting slush and sticky mud while pulling heavy wagons and being fed smaller than normal rations began to take a toll. Finally, within a few weeks, some fresh grass peeked through the melting snow, and the travelers let the horses enjoy the first sweet taste of spring.

The wagons showed the wear and tear of the journey too. Sometimes a damaged wheel or a broken axle would make a wagon unrepairable, and its owners, along with only their most valued items, had to be parceled out to other wagons, with most of their remaining possessions left behind.

As they plodded along one mid-March day, the wagons in front of the Muellers came to a halt. Rolf was managing the team of their wagon, as he usually did, and he tried to lean out to see why Detlef and the others were stopping. Suddenly there was shouting, and Rolf jumped down to see what was going on. He quickly jumped back on the wagon and said in a loud whisper, "Partisans!"

Johanna told everyone to sit still and remain quiet. "How many did you see?"

"Several, maybe fifteen or so."

Georg, who was sitting behind them in the wagon, tried to figure out why fifteen Partisans could be a problem for wagons full of Germans, then he realized the Partisans would be armed, and the travelers would have little chance against them.

One group had stopped at the Pöhlmanns' wagon just a couple ahead of Detlef's. Again, there was an angry shout. It was in Czech, but the meaning was clear. They were ordering Günter to get down. Rolf leaned out to see what was happening. It appeared Günter hadn't understood the man's broken German, so the Partisan repeated the command, and then when Günter didn't respond, one of them got off his horse and pulled Günter off the wagon, causing him to lose his balance. As he struggled to get up, the man kicked him, then the others joined in, and soon they were beating the hell out of poor Günter Pöhlmann, with his wife and Minna watching and screaming for someone to come to his aid. Everyone sat there watching Günter get beaten, knowing he might not survive, yet afraid to respond for fear they'd get what Günter was getting or worse.

Suddenly there was another commotion in the far distance. It was a detachment of Germans who'd been assigned to watch the roads and keep refugees safe, and they were speeding toward the caravan. When the Partisans saw them coming, they fled the scene, with the Germans in pursuit. The Partisans had enough of a head start that they were able to reach the nearby woods, and with their knowledge of the terrain, they soon made it to safety. The Germans gave up pursuit and came to check on the people in the wagons. When they came to check on Günter, they just shook their heads and said there wasn't much they could do, then they moved on and began checking on the others.

Johanna ordered Rolf to stay with Georg while she and Annelise ran to where Olexa and Minna were kneeling by Günter. He was badly beaten, his right eye swollen shut, with blood coming from his mouth and cuts on his face, and he kept passing out from pain. His breathing was ragged, and he winced with each breath from the damage to his ribs. Minna was screaming and crying at the same time, and Olexa was trying to calm her while attending to Günter.

Annelise put her arms around Minna and comforted her while Johanna knelt next to Olexa to see what she could do to help. She was shocked at the extent of Günter's injuries and doubted he could survive them.

Other people began to gather around, some out of genuine concern, a few out of morbid curiosity, and Johanna yelled at them, "Please get us some water!" Two women left to take care of that.

Olexa came out of her daze and told Minna and Annelise to fetch an old shirt from the wagon. They could use it to clean and bandage. It was good for Minna, because having something to do helped calm her. When they came back with the shirt, another couple came with a bucket of water, which Olexa used to clean her husband's wounds. As she was wiping his face, he woke up, looking confused for a moment. He tried to sit up, but the pain was overwhelming, and he quickly gave up the effort. A few minutes later, he tried again, this time with the assistance of one of the men. He was wobbly, even sitting, and the man sat behind him with his back against Günter's, helping to keep him upright.

Günter whispered, "I could use some of that water."

Minna ran to get a cup and filled it from the water bucket. Günter sipped it slowly, and it was obvious that even swallowing was painful.

Several minutes later, the crowd had thinned, leaving only Johanna, Annelise, and the Lehmanns to help the Pöhlmanns, and there was noise among them that indicated they were preparing to move on. Günter said, "I need to get up. I need to be able to walk or ride in the wagon. We must keep up." He doubted the wagons would wait for them, and if left alone, he and his family would be easy pickings for another Partisan attack. His holding them back might result in their deaths.

Johanna was concerned. "Are you sure you're ready?"

"I have to be."

She understood his meaning and asked, "How can we help you?"

"Perhaps Rolf and Detlef can assist me."

Rolf and Detlef each knelt beside Günter so that he could put his arms over their shoulders. They slowly stood with Günter, and they managed to get him on his feet. The effort was almost too much, and although he was standing, there was little optimism he'd be able to travel. Rolf and Detlef soon felt him getting weaker. Rolf looked at his Uncle Detlef, amazed that he had the strength to help but glad to have his help just the same.

Another man came to them. He'd been among the group that was standing around earlier. "I've checked with all the other wagons, and there's no doctor with us. I'm sorry."

Günter sighed. "I suppose some schnapps would be the next best thing if anyone has some."

"I have some in my wagon, if you'd like."

"I think I would. Maybe it would kill the pain."

The man went and returned with a half-filled bottle of schnapps. Günter took a healthy swallow, coughed at the harshness of the homemade liquor, then thanked the man. In a few minutes, he seemed to be a little better, so perhaps the schnapps had helped.

Olexa asked him if he thought he could make it inside the wagon to sleep while they resumed their trip. After sizing up the situation, he told her he would try.

It was excruciatingly painful for Günter and difficult for the men, but they helped him inside and made a bed for him on the floor of the wagon, with every available blanket put there to shield him from the rough ride he'd have to endure. Olexa took the reins, and the wagons started moving again. It was a long and unbearable afternoon for Günter, and that night was not much better.

The next day, Günter thought walking might be less painful, but by late morning he was exhausted, so when the wagons stopped for a brief rest at lunch, he took to the floor of the wagon again. It was brutal, but he took another sip of schnapps, and that helped him endure the pain.

Günter Pöhlmann had a tremendous will, and he could stand more pain than almost any man, but there were times it was so much he thought he would have been better off if the Partisans had finished their work. But he knew he had to be strong for Olexa and Minna. Each day, he walked for a longer period before becoming exhausted, and only a few days later, he sat on the wagon seat, taking the reins from his wife. He still looked thin and pale, and it was easy to see that by the end of each day the pain had become almost unbearable again.

There came another warm day they were making good progress, so when they found a good place to stop not too far off the road, they made camp early. While the adults were busy starting fires and preparing food, Georg took advantage of their inattention and wandered off. He made it back to the road to check out a detachment of German soldiers standing and watching at a junction. He thought they might be the men who'd come to their rescue a few days earlier, so he went to talk with them.

They were a different crew, but Georg, always comfortable around soldiers, struck up a conversation, and they were amused at his boldness. He asked why they were standing there and learned they had been assigned to check the papers of travelers on the two roads. They asked him if his parents knew where he was, and he told them he was traveling with his mother only, since his father was a soldier fighting the Russians. The soldiers exchanged glances, then one of them said he hoped Georg would see his father soon.

Just as he finished saying that, they heard a motorcycle approaching. The soldier motioned for Georg to return to the camp, but the boy only went a few feet away. He was fascinated with the men and wanted to talk to them some more after they were finished checking the identification of the men on the motorcycle. There were three riders, two on the cycle and one of them in a sidecar. The Germans were all business, with their guns at the ready, and their leader held up his hand signaling the three men to stop. They coasted to him, stopping just as they reached him. He asked them for their identification, and they produced their papers. They didn't talk much as the leader checked their documents, handed them back, then directed them to proceed.

Georg watched the men make it about twenty-five meters, when the leader pulled up his weapon and fired a burst of bullets, striking all three of them within seconds. The motorcycle careened off the road and landed on its side in a ditch. The man lowered his gun, then directed two of his men to go check and make sure no one was alive. They walked slowly with guns trained on the men in the ditch. When they reached them, there was one additional shot, ending the life of the only survivor. As they walked back, the man who'd done the shooting turned and saw Georg standing there with a stunned look on his face. "These men were Partisans. They won't trouble anyone now."

Georg wondered how the man knew that, but he was too stunned to ask. No longer wanting to talk to the soldiers, he started back to his wagon, walking slowly at first. He turned back at one point to see if the men were watching, but they were talking among themselves and laughing. How could they laugh after that? He took off running, wanting to get back to his family and as far from what he'd just seen as he could. When he arrived, he received a scolding from his mother for wandering off. He just stood there with an expressionless face, offering no explanations or excuses. When she looked at her son, Johanna could tell something had happened. "Where have you been, Georg, and what have you seen?"

Tears started coming down his cheeks, which worried his mother. She insisted he tell her. Between sobs, he related what he'd witnessed, and when he finished, Johanna gasped, then grabbed her youngest son and pulled him to her. "Don't wander off again, do you hear me?"

"I won't."

Johanna hung on to Georg, thinking how many horrible things her youngest child had already witnessed and praying there would be no more of them. But it was only a few days later that more trouble came. As they traveled that day, they began to hear sounds of war, including artillery, and as the day grew late the sounds grew louder. As night fell they could see the flashes from the big guns growing ever closer, and they knew they could be in harm's way.

There were woods to their right, so people started abandoning their wagons and heading for whatever safety those trees would provide. The Mueller family didn't make it to the woods, finding safety behind a berm. When shells started falling in the woods, people started fleeing. One older lady said, "I am too old for this," and she stood up. Before anyone could talk her back down, she fell dead from a stray bullet. No one could understand her actions. She would have been safe if she had just stayed down.

Luckily for the surviving refugees, the firing stopped several hours later, with none of the wagons damaged and their horses unhurt. They later learned that the Russians had caught up with the Freiwillige Galizien, a volunteer division made up of Ukrainians. The war had found the wagon train, and it was horrific. The urgency to make it to safety grew among all the refugees. For Johanna, the horror of that night—with cannons firing and shells flying overhead—made Herman's ordeal more real to her and raised her level of concern for him even higher.

It was a few nights later that Johanna had a terrible dream. She sat up straight, waking her children as she did. "Did you hear that?"

"What, Mother?"

"That explosion?"

None of the three youngsters had heard anything. Annelise said, "It must have been a nightmare, Mother."

Johanna thought for a moment, then realized she'd been dreaming, and in that dream, she had been talking to Herman, who was standing in front of her, dressed in his gear. There was a blinding light and an explosion, which must have awakened her.

"Yes, it must have been a dream. I'm sorry, go back to sleep."

She fretted about the dream for days after that, worrying it was an omen that something terrible had happened to her husband. What she didn't know was that only a few days earlier, Herman and his young companion had been in a position that had come under heavy bombardment. Every time a shell exploded, they checked to see that the men around them were unharmed. Then came a shell whose flash they saw and sound they heard at the exact instant the shrapnel tore through their position.

✦ 24 ✦

The Final Leg

March 1945

Some of the families started running low on food by late March. Other families, especially those from farms, had bigger stores of supplies to draw from, and those families were asked to help the families who'd begun to run out. As the needy came by their wagon, Johanna became conflicted. She knew they still had a few days of travel ahead, followed by the uncertainty of what might be available to them in Germany, so she wanted to make sure there would still be food for her family when they got to German soil. When those hungry children kept coming to her it was hard for her to say no, so she compromised and gave them some food, telling their parents that the food was only for the children. Some parents followed her wishes, while others got only a few meters away before insisting the children share. So the next day, Johanna relented and doled out food to the adults as well as the children. It was a move of practicality as much as benevolence. Hungry people will do what is needed to get food, so sharing was better than fighting them off, risking the loss of it all.

When they made it to Austria in April, two full months after first setting out, there was a feeling of relief at being on German-held soil, but no great celebration. Chances were less now of being attacked by Partisans, so there was that to be grateful for, but everyone knew the war would soon be over, and no one could be certain what awaited them when that day came. The group stayed together, thinking it better to do that than risk going into areas where battles might be raging.

It was during this interval that Johanna sat with Detlef and Elsa after breakfast and talked about where they should go when the time came to move.

"I think Detlef and I would like to go see our parents near Dresden. It's been so long since we've seen them. They're getting older, and I'm sure they could use our help."

"Elsa, the Russians have taken over that part of Germany. Are you sure you want to travel into an area they control?"

"Where else is there, Johanna? Come with us, please."

"No, we could never live under Russian control. Herman would never allow it. I'm going to Frankfurt. Peter and his wife are there, and Herman suggested going there in his letter. Herman will know we're not in Strednitz. Where else in a country as large as Germany would he look, if not Frankfurt?"

Elsa and Detlef exchanged glances. While they wanted to believe Herman was alive, they were no longer as sure of it as Johanna seemed to be, and there were times after one of her bad dreams, even Johanna had doubts. Johanna saw the glances and realized why they weren't responding. "I must believe he's still alive, Elsa! I can't think any other way." Then, she covered her face with her hand and fought back tears.

Elsa tried to comfort her sister.

After a few minutes, Johanna regained control. "To be honest I had a terrible dream again last night, and it was the worst yet. I was at the same field where I would see Herman, but he wasn't there this time. No one was, and it was quiet. There were no birds singing, no trees nor grass nor flowers—nothing was alive, and I heard only the wind blowing." The tears came faster, and Elsa hugged her sister. Johanna leaned into the comforting arms of her sister and said, "I don't like to think what that means."

Elsa wasn't one to believe in premonitions, but the dream got her thinking that Herman was lost to them and that something inside Johanna was preparing her for the awful news.

They sat there until Johanna once again regained control. "It's time to clean up." As they rose to do that, they saw a man walking toward them. He was dirty and had on a ragged, disheveled uniform. His left hand and lower arm were heavily bandaged.

Rolf was the first to recognize him. He yelled, "Father!" and ran to him. He almost knocked Herman over as he wrapped his arms around him, and Herman gave a slight grunt of pain. Soon, Johanna and the other children were there, hugging and crying for joy.

After a moment, Johanna stepped back to look at him again and saw the bandages. "You're hurt!"

"Yes. I caught some shrapnel in my hand, and they had to operate to remove most of it. There are still some pieces in there, but not as many as before, and the pain is less. Thank God it was only my hand."

Detlef and Elsa arrived to join the happy group, with Emma beating them by a few steps. As they greeted him, Detlef eyed Herman's injured hand with an odd expression. Herman explained that it was shrapnel, and there was a story behind it he would share with them on another day. Detlef's expression changed now that he no longer thought Herman's wound might have been self-inflicted.

"Come, dear Herman, we've just eaten breakfast. You must be starved."

"I am, and I'd be happy to get out of these clothes. They don't smell the best!"

"I brought some of yours with me," Johanna replied.

"I knew you would." Then Herman kissed his wife, and while they kissed, all the danger and difficulty they'd just endured and all the uncertainty that lay ahead disappeared. There was only that moment and that kiss.

They hardly gave Herman time to eat. There was so much they wanted to know, and Johanna began the questioning, asking how he found them there in Austria, of all places.

"I knew you would have left Czechoslovakia, and given where the Russians were, you'd most likely come this way, so I just kept walking and checking with groups until I was told by someone that a large group had stopped here. Somehow, I knew I'd find you among them."

Detlef looked at Herman, seeing a man who had faced the horrors of the front line, who'd been injured in battle, who had walked countless miles to find them, and he held admiration for his brother-in-law. "You're a smart man and a brave one, Herman Mueller."

"And a lucky one today."

Detlef nodded. "It will all be better now."

"I hope so, Detlef, and I can't thank you enough for all you've done to help get my family to safety."

Detlef smiled at the compliment. "It was nothing more than I should do."

"Still, it was appreciated."

Detlef fidgeted for moment, then said, "To be honest, more of the credit goes to Johanna and Elsa than to me."

"I'm sure everyone pitched in."

"And while I'm being completely honest, you should be proud of your Annelise and Rolf. Our Emma, too, for that matter. They did more than should be expected of young people."

Herman nodded, his eyes brimming. "I'm so proud of all of them—of all of you—and so grateful to be with you again."

"As I said, things will be better now."

Herman considered their situation. They were together again, but essentially homeless with no clear path to a future. "At least we're reunited. We'll take what comes next and make the best of it."

He finally finished his breakfast and asked Johanna for the change of clothes. He took them to a nearby stream, where he rid himself of every shred of military garb, washed himself in the icy water, and got dressed. He returned to their wagon and asked Johanna to fashion a new bandage for him. When she changed the bandage, she saw how extensive his wounds were and watched as he plucked a couple of pieces of shrapnel that had just emerged from his wounds.

That night was unseasonably warm, and Johanna asked the three children if they'd like to sleep on the ground outside the crowded wagon. They thought sleeping under the stars would be fun, so Herman and Johanna had the wagon to themselves, the two of them together for the first time in more than a year.

25

The War Ends

June 1945

By the time the war came to an end, their band of wagons had joined a group on German soil near the Danube. There were nearly a thousand wagons filled with refugee families, all of them waiting and pondering where to go next and what they would do when they made it there. The refugees were in an area occupied by American troops, and for the most part the relationship between them and the Americans was amicable.

Around their encampment there were piles of weapons, and when no adults were watching young boys combed through them and pocketed any bullets they found for souvenirs. Then came the night one of the boys paid a price for doing that. He and his family were sitting near a campfire when something, perhaps the heat of the fire or a spark that landed on his clothing, caused the bullet to explode. At that precise moment Georg was walking by. He heard the pop of the bullet, then heard the boy's agonized screams and the panicked shouts of his parents. He could hear the mother begging for a doctor and then saw people running through the camp asking for one. He remembered there was no doctor for Günter when he was beaten by the Partisans, but there were more wagons now, and he hoped there would be a doctor among them to help the boy.

When Georg got back to his parents, they asked him where he'd gone, and he told them he'd been on a walk. Herman asked, "Were you near where all the noise was coming from?"

He answered that he was.

"What did you see?"

"I didn't see anything. I just heard a loud pop, and then there was lots of screaming and yelling. I think a friend might have gotten hurt."

Herman decided he'd go see if he could be of any help. Several minutes later he returned. He stood over Georg and said, "The boy had a bullet in his pocket. Something made it go off. He's badly hurt."

Georg looked at his feet. "I was with him when he found the bullet."

Herman put his hands on Georg's shoulders. "And did you find a bullet?"

Still looking down, he said, "Yes, Father."

"And where is it?"

"In my pocket."

"May I see it?"

Georg reached in and pulled out not one, but three bullets. Johanna gasped.

Herman said, "Give them to me, Son," and Georg did as he was told.

Herman paused a moment, then went to the edge of the woods and threw them as far as he could.

He turned back to Georg. "Don't ever do that again. Do you understand?"

"Yes, Father."

Georg stared at his feet again, hating that his father, so recently united with them, was upset with him. Johanna called Georg to her, and knowing from her voice she would be a source of comfort, he hurried to her. She wrapped her arms around his shoulders and held him to her. Georg sensed something in that hug, and he backed away. "Do you think my friend will live?"

Johanna gently put her fingers under his chin and lifted his face toward hers. "There's no way of knowing. You must say a prayer for him tonight before you go to sleep."

"I will."

She held her son close again, and her thoughts went to the mother whose family had gotten this far, only to have this happen. *The war is over. Will there never be an end to the pain?*

Later that evening as Herman lay next to Johanna in the wagon, he could feel her restlessness. "Are you okay?"

"That could have been our Georg tonight."

"I know."

"The difference between being happy and sad is so small sometimes, and it's all so—what's the word for it—*willkürlich*. And such randomness is, by its nature, unfair." He raised up, leaning on his elbow. "This has all made me think of the night I was wounded, and I think it's time I tell you about it."

"Herman, I've never asked about that night because I wasn't sure I wanted to hear your answer. Hearing about it would have told me how close

I was to losing you."

"I wasn't the one who might have died that night. It was Heinrich, the young man who lay next to me in the bunker. He was the one to worry about.

"The shells came in from the Russian guns for hours that day. We called them *Ratsch-Bum* because you would hear the buzzing noise first, then the explosion. Shell after shell hit around us. Some hit the positions of our friends and took them instantly. Others hit nearby, and with those it was the shrapnel that would kill or injure. It was as you say, by chance."

She gently took his injured hand in hers. "And this was how you were injured?"

"Yes."

"I'm thankful it was only your hand, but how did it happen that it wasn't more than this?"

"After endless hours of shelling, a person would go through different stages of fear and shock, and then sometimes you would just become numb to it all, and you didn't care what happened."

"Yes?" *So did my Herman raise his hand, hoping to be hurt that night? Is that what happened?* Johanna wondered.

He could read her thoughts. "I thought of you and held on, and then the shelling stopped for a time. Young Heinrich thought it was over, and when I looked over I could see he was starting to move, and then I heard the buzzing of another shell coming in. I yelled at him and started to reach over to push his head down to safety, but he heard me and ducked. He was safe, but my hand was in the air when the shell exploded."

"You tried to save him."

"I did, but soon after that I was sent for medical attention, leaving him there. I knew I might get sent home because of my wounded hand, and of course that thought made me happy, but I worried about the young Heinrich. He'd left behind a young bride who was expecting their baby, and I wanted him to make it home to them. If I weren't there with him, I couldn't help him anymore. Did he survive so that he'd get to see his bride and baby? This I'll never know."

He grew quiet, thinking of the uncertainty of wartime and how unfair it was that so many had died. Herman was glad he'd been spared so that he could make it home to his wife and family, and he hoped the young man had made it home, too, but there was a good chance he might not have. There were hundreds of thousands of German soldiers who never made it home, and for each one of them there were dozens of enemy soldiers and innocent civilians who lost their lives as well, and all of it the result of the insane megalomania of a man and his underlings.

Herman was seldom a man to think too deeply of things. He was pragmatic, thinking only of what needed to be done to get through each day. That night his mind went to everything that had happened since they'd been forced to leave Tariverde. He thought of the men who were responsible for it all, his mind dwelling on the horrors he'd witnessed on the Russian Front. Johanna pulled him close to her as his sobs wracked his body. After that evening, Herman was stoic again and full of purpose, and those few moments of grief and regret were the only ones he allowed himself.

$\backsim$ 26 $\sim$

Refugees Again

July 1945

A few weeks later, after a warm summer day, Georg lay sleeping on the ground when he was awakened by a hand covering his mouth. He tried to squirm free and yell out for help, but the person was too strong and wouldn't let him. Who was this stranger, and what had he done to his family? Then he heard a whisper. "It's your father. Be quiet, and I will take my hand away." Relieved to hear his father's voice, Georg shook his head yes. He could see very little in the dark, but he sensed that everyone else was awake. "We're leaving tonight, Son. Get dressed."

Georg did as he was told, getting dressed and putting on his shoes while his family gathered up a few things from the wagon. Then as quietly as they could, the Muellers set out on foot. Their horses, the wagon, much of their food, and most of their remaining possessions were left behind.

Somehow Herman had learned that the territory they were in was to be turned over to the Russians under an agreement made among the Allied leaders before the war had ended. He had no desire to be under Russian control, so he decided to leave that night. He tried to persuade Detlef and Elsa to come with them, but to no avail. Detlef was sure they could make it to Dresden. They told no one else, because to do so would have created a mass exodus, and they would have been stopped.

They managed to make their way to an unguarded bridge, then crossed the Danube. The better roads were on the other side of the river, but they found a path along their side. At first the path was wide and easy to travel, but it soon became narrow and overgrown. They made their way through on that moonless night until they came to a tributary, swift and swollen with the melting snow of the Alps. It would have been dangerous to cross, so they had to make their way up the stream until they found a safer place to ford. Once they'd crossed it, they followed a narrow path with only starlight showing their way and returned to the path along the Danube, because following it would lead them to safety. They repeated the process as they encountered other streams. Progress was slow that night.

When daylight came, they could see the Danube, also running high with snowmelt. Oftentimes they would see bodies bobbing in the current, a reminder to be vigilant as they made their way along the riverbank. Several of the bodies wore the uniforms of German soldiers whose deaths were due more to choice than chance.

For days, they kept moving west through Bavaria, normally a beautiful region of Germany, but not quite so for refugees on the run. As the days passed, their situation became more dire. The once-proud Mueller family was homeless and running out of food, and when the day came they had finished the last of it, Johanna asked, "What will we do now, Herman?"

"We'll find a way."

"Have you not heard them, Herman? They call us Flüchtlinge now, and the way they say it sounds as if we aren't refugees fleeing the Russians, but Gypsies like the ones we used to ridicule."

"I'll find a way to feed my family!"

"I hope you will. You're the one who has us in this predicament. We could be with my sister and her family. We could be with the others, but you had us flee. You had us leave everything. So yes, Herman. I hope you have a way to get us food at least!"

The children were stunned. Of course they had seen their parents disagree before, but they'd never seen their mother speak to their father in the way she spoke to him that day. Herman stood there with a mix of anger and resignation, because Johanna had a point. He'd been the one to force his family to flee the Russians, but he was also the one who'd spent months facing the Russian army, fighting them, hating them, fearing them. He was the one with the wounded hand that might mark him as a soldier. If that happened, he could have been taken from his loved ones and sent somewhere awful, or worse yet, they might all have been sent with him and none of them heard from again.

Johanna had heard these worries on the night they fled the camp, but on the day when the food was gone, she wondered if it would have been worse to stay with the others rather than flee. She knew Herman felt he had to make the choice he did, but at that moment Herman was the immediate cause for everything that had gone wrong in their lives. She was angry with him but equally upset with herself for blaming him.

He searched for words to reassure her. "I will find some work. I won't let you starve."

She looked at him and wanted to go to him, to hold him and tell him she was sorry for her sharp words, but she couldn't. Maybe soon. Maybe when things were better. But not that day. Not when her children were hungry and there was no prospect of food.

Starving people must give up their principles and do whatever is required to feed their children, and there were hordes of starving people in Germany in those days. The Muellers sought help all along the way. Some people were kind to them and provided a tidbit here and there, much as Johanna had done to the people without food during the last stages of their journey, but there were too many to feed, and the generous ones had their own families to provide for. The few handouts helped, but they were never enough.

When several days had passed with very little food, the Muellers had to resort to tactics they would never have dreamed possible before. If people said no to Herman's offer to do work in exchange for food, then other means were required.

They found ways to steal or beg for some grams of flour, or an apple or two. Georg found seed potatoes uncovered in the fields under moonlight and ate them with just a slight brushing of the dirt. He learned how to steal bread here and there and became quite adept at it. He felt ashamed, but it was something he had to do. Had it been just him, maybe it would have been easy to give up, but looking at the faces of his starving family, he did what he had to do. If there was a half-loaf of bread, he would have that bread. If there were two apples, he would have them, too, and make sure his family had something to eat.

When they had food given to them by kind strangers, or as payment for work Herman would do, or if that food was a result of theft, the parents always made sure to feed the children first. Johanna waited for them to eat, and Herman, too, before she would allow herself to eat. There were times she lied to Herman that she had eaten just so he would eat, and if there was nothing left, at least her loved ones had eaten. Georg knew his mother hadn't eaten, but a look from her told him not to tell. He and Johanna had a bond during those days. Herman, Annelise, and Rolf were above stealing food, but not above eating it when Johanna and Georg found a way to procure it.

Layered on top of their hunger was a sense of hopelessness. It was one thing to go without food for a time, but quite another to have no idea if one would get food or where it would come from. Starvation and fear have always been a bad combination. When the weather turned bad, as it did sometimes, with rain pouring on them and no real shelter, their misery reached new depths. Still they kept moving west, finding just enough food to survive and hoping their luck would improve.

After weeks of this, they made their way to an industrial town near the Danube called Regensburg. Herman heard of a farmer who might need help, and he convinced the man to take him on as a worker. The man agreed to take him on, and the period of starvation came to an end. They had a roof over their heads, they had food to eat, and their clothes were clean. The children even attended Catholic schools for two months. It was a respite from their period of want, but they knew it wouldn't last forever, and sure enough, within weeks the farmer had no more work for Herman and had to let him go. Once again the Mueller family was forced to move in search of food and shelter.

✺ 27 ✻

Happenbach, Germany

Fall 1945

They thanked the farmer for giving them a place to stay and food to eat, then, using money Johanna had saved and sewn into her clothing, they bought a horse and wagon. It wasn't much, but it improved their mobility and their prospects. They made their way west through Nuremburg to Happenbach, a small village of two hundred in Baden-Württemberg. It was there that another opportunity awaited Herman. He became part of a highway work crew.

They were assigned a small apartment over a restaurant. The apartment consisted of a small kitchen, a living space, and one bedroom. It wasn't much of a residence, but compared to their nomadic days spent in search of food and shelter, the small, cramped apartment was a haven.

Herman's pay was meager, and Johanna looked for ways to stretch their income. Rolf, fourteen by then, was placed in an apprenticeship at a plant nursery, and Annelise, sixteen, was placed with a family to help manage their household. Apprenticeships were four-year commitments. The first year, the two of them were paid next to nothing, with only slight increases during the second and third years. The fourth year, having learned their trades, they would be qualified to earn full salaries. Whatever small piece of childhood had been left to Annelise and Rolf Mueller disappeared as they entered those apprenticeships. Ready for it or not, they had entered the world of adults.

Only Georg had it good in Happenbach, and the time in the village marked the happiest years of his young life. There were several other boys his age, and they ran together, playing as children should play. The small Bach that gave the village its name was dammed by the boys, and the resulting pool of water provided them a place to swim. When winter came, the boys fashioned ice skates out of triangular pieces of wood strapped to their shoes with number nine wire, and they skated on the frozen pond.

When they weren't swimming or skating, they found a hundred other ways to have fun, and many of those got them in trouble. The boys loved to play hide-and-seek in the wheat fields, but of course their play caused extensive damage to the crops. Farmers would chase the boys out of the fields, and the ones who were unlucky enough to get caught received a good scolding and oftentimes a swat or two. The farmers understood that boys would be boys and forgave them the next day. The boys' parents held no grudges against the farmers, feeling the boys deserved their punishments.

When the boys weren't in the fields, chances were they'd be climbing fruit and walnut trees like a band of primates, picking the trees clean in a matter of minutes and damaging branches as they did. Again, punishments would result for the ones who got caught.

They found dozens of ways to spend their time, including badger hunting. They would block the hole to an animal's den and try to smoke it out, but never with any success.

When badger hunting failed, their attention often turned to the wasps that nested in the ground and stung unsuspecting people who stepped on those nests or ran over them with their wagons. One of the boys' favorite pastimes was eliminating those hives. Stores sold sticks impregnated with sulfur for a few pfennigs. The boys would take handfuls of mud, light the sulfur stick, put it into the hole of the hive, then place the mud on top of the hole and run like hell. The wasps, with no means of escape, were killed by the sulfur fumes, and the returning wasps would be killed one by one as they landed and looked for the entrance to their nest.

That would have been fun in and of itself, but the city government of Abstatt, an organized village a kilometer away, offered a reward of fifty pfennigs to those who brought in the nests with the dead wasps. The boys came upon a nest one day, and the attraction of the reward was too much. They followed the regimen with the sulfur and the mud, then proudly took the nest to Abstatt City Hall, where they were given their reward. They had no sooner split the reward and left the office than they heard the shrieks of the office staff. It seemed the nest was occupied by a hardy group of wasps who hadn't been killed—only stunned. The wasps were waking up, and they weren't happy with what had transpired, so they took out their anger on the mayor and secretaries. Soon after that day, the location for turning in the wasp nests was changed, and everyone from Happenbach to Abstatt knew who to blame.

Herman's job with the road crew was repairing damage done to the bridges on the autobahn during the German army's retreat toward Berlin. It was difficult work, but a job, nonetheless. One of the features that made it more pleasant was that the workers received two breaks each day, with one at 10 a.m. and one again at 3 p.m., and the workers were allowed to drink beer while on break.

Georg and his friends learned of this and picked the lock to the shed where the beer and tools were stored. The tools were left untouched, but they drank all the beer. Herman and the other fathers learned who was responsible and soon taught the boys that drinking their fathers' work beer was not a good idea.

Happenbach was a true farming community. The families had between five and fifteen acres of land each. The homes were two stories, with the cattle living on the first level and the families above them. Attached to the homes were barns where the hay was stored, and next to the barns were piles of manure. Each farmer had a small vineyard, with land left over for food crops for the people and grain and hay for the animals. The farms were small and the families couldn't afford machinery, so their animals provided the power needed for planting and harvesting.

When spring came, music returned to Happenbach, but the instruments weren't ones found in orchestras. The music came from hammers striking anvils. With there being no machinery, the farmers used scythes and sickles in the fields, and they got dull with repeated use. In other places, men might have grinders or files to sharpen their tools. In Happenbach, the men laid their tools atop anvils and sharpened them with hammer blows, creating a nightly symphony heard throughout the village until late in the fall.

There was a milk house in the middle of town to which the farmers would bring milk to be cooled and sold. Some of the milk was sold to local families, but most of it went to a dairy business that came by to collect it.

Attached to the milk house was a Backhaus that was open all the time and was a gathering place for Georg and his friends until the teenagers took it over in the evening. A fire was built in the bakehouse, and then, when the bricks were heated and the ashes were cleaned out, wonderful treats such as pies and bread were placed on large wooden spatulas and shoved inside to be baked. The boys couldn't wait for the treats to come out, because nothing ever tasted better.

Some days after the wheat had been harvested, Georg would be required to accompany his mother as she walked the wheat fields picking up the stray wheat ears left on the ground. In late summer, gathering beech nuts in the woods was another task requiring his help. The nuts were found among the leaves, collected in baskets, and pressed into cooking oil to be used the rest of the year. Georg hated both of those tasks and resented the fact that his family was so poor they had to resort to gathering food in fields and woods. But there was a day his thinking changed. A young girl named Klara joined them in the woods, along with her mother. They were refugees like the Muellers, and Klara was the prettiest girl Georg had ever seen. He was smitten with her and dreamed of her in the way young boys dream of their first loves.

Most of Georg's friends had bicycles, and he constantly begged his parents to get him one. They promised they would when they could find one they could afford. Georg found a couple he loved, but their owners wanted too much for them. So when Herman managed to trade some work for one that was used but well taken care of, Georg was elated. Johanna was less so. She had to stretch their budget to buy the necessities, and they could have used the money Herman had bypassed. She was also concerned that a place might have to be found for it in their small apartment, but Herman had already arranged with a neighbor to store it in his barn. Hearing that and seeing how happy Georg was, Johanna relented.

There came a day in 1948 that Georg sat on that bicycle, waiting for three friends who had agreed to cycle across Germany to Lake Constance and then sail across it to Switzerland. Georg was only twelve, but a couple of the others were older, so his parents agreed he could go and even gave him twenty marks for the trip.

His friends were late that day, and after he had waited at the designated meeting point for them to show, he rode to one of their houses to see what was delaying them. When he made it to the front door, his friend came out, looking a bit surprised to see him. "Did you not hear, Georg? We can't go."

"Obviously not. I have my gear on the back of my bicycle and money in my pocket for the trip."

"I'm sorry. I guess each of us thought one of the others had told you. Maybe some other time. Maybe when we're a little older—maybe then our parents will let us go."

"But my parents have already said I could go."

"Your parents are the best! None of ours would agree to let us."

Georg was angry, and he knew if he talked to his friend much longer, he'd grow even more so. He stared instead at his foot on the bike pedal, wondering what to do.

"Again, I'm sorry, and maybe another time we can do this."

Georg looked up at his friend. "I'm going without you. I'll see you when I get back."

"By yourself! You're twelve! It's over two hundred kilometers! I wouldn't . . ."

"Well I would, and I am. I'll see you soon."

"Okay. Be safe."

And with that, young Georg Mueller turned around and headed out for the long ride south. He should have gone home and told his parents he was going alone, but they would have forbidden him to go. His young mind told him it would be better to be reprimanded on his return than to be told he couldn't go.

He cycled across Baden-Württemberg, in shorts and shirtless most days. It was summer after all. He stayed in youth hostels. He bought loaves of rye bread and wurst to keep hunger at bay. He picked fruit off the trees along the right of way. And then, after a few days, he made it to the shores of Lake Constance. The beautiful lake issued an invitation to ferry across it and set foot in Switzerland, just so he could brag to his friends that he'd accomplished what they couldn't.

He made the trip across the lake and spent a little time on Swiss soil before beginning the long ride home. Days later, he arrived home to find his parents both relieved and angry, and his friends envious of his adventure.

Georg attended the local school with his friends, and once again all the students were taught in a single room. It was a better situation than in Vysoka though, and the teachers tended to stay for longer periods. In 1948 a high school was built in Bielstein, eight kilometers from Happenbach, and it was there that Georg and his friends were sent to continue their education.

High school was quite different from elementary school. Students stayed in the same room with different teachers rotating in for each subject. During his first year, Georg did well in every class except for English, for him a foreign language. The next year he was required to take French and it joined English as a class with poor marks. As that year progressed his worries grew, because to fail a subject would mean the end of his education. When the last day came he had good marks in geography, math, and science. When he received his mark in English, it was a 4, just above failing.

Then came the last class of the day, French. He wasn't alone in worrying. Several other students knew they were at risk just as he was. The teacher handed out their report cards and Georg could easily tell those who'd passed and those who hadn't. Finally, the instructor handed Georg his grade card. He could hardly bear to look, and when he did, his heart fell. He'd failed French. The students had been told that failing meant they could not return when fall came. At the age of fourteen, Georg's career in public education in Germany had come to an end. By fall, with his father's assistance, he would be a carpenter's apprentice.

✑ 28 ✑

Thoughts of Leaving

January 1952

While many of his friends returned to school, Georg learned the trade of carpentry. There was no more running the village and the fields with the boys, getting into mischief. It was time now for long days of hard work. His entry into the working world meant that all five members of the Mueller family were now employed, but prosperity still eluded them.

Postwar Germany held little promise for men like Herman Mueller and their families. His highway job had ended after six months, and Herman had to settle for a factory job in nearby Heilbronn. Not long after that, Johanna, too, found work there. Their combined earnings were still minimal, and they never earned enough to move out of the small apartment. It was a far cry from their days in Tariverde and Strednitz, and it made them yearn for something better.

Herman had thought of leaving Germany since their first days in Happenbach. Times were hard in postwar Germany, so he looked abroad for opportunities. He sought to emigrate to Argentina, Uruguay, Paraguay, Canada, and South Africa with no luck. In desperation he'd even written a letter to Haile Selassie of Ethiopia. When he told Johanna that he'd done that, she was incredulous. "Ethiopia! What kind of life would we have there?"

"I've heard good things about it, and what do we have here in Happenbach? Rolf is stuck at a nursery. He does the best he can, but he sees no future there. Annelise is nothing more than a servant in that household, and we hardly ever see her. Our Georg is doing the work of a man, and you and I—what future do we have going to Heilbronn each day and working long hours for little pay?"

Johanna was frustrated that Herman couldn't find better work in Germany. She'd moved enough, but she was pragmatic and understood that if there was nothing for them in Germany, then they had to search elsewhere. "Try America then."

Herman sent letters to the United States but got no response. Then in 1951, Rolf came to his parents and asked to talk with them. When the three of them were seated in the kitchen, Rolf announced, "I'm ready to leave Happenbach."

Herman looked at his son and realized he was no longer a boy. Rolf was twenty-one, a man now, and he was unhappy. Herman knew his son was old enough to make his own decisions, but that decision would tear the family apart, so he asked, "Without us?"

Rolf stared at his father, unblinking and determined. "If that's the only way, then yes, without you."

"Where would you go, Rolf?"

"My friend has found a way to Canada. I'm going to try to join him."

Johanna spoke out. "You won't go without us!"

Rolf looked at his mother, then back at Herman. "If you want me to be with you, you'll need to come to Canada too."

It grew quiet in the kitchen. Rolf sat straight in his chair with his arms crossed in front of him. Herman and Johanna could tell he was serious, and if they didn't take some action to forestall him, they would see their son leave them.

"Give me another few months, Rolf. I'll redouble my efforts and find a place we can all go. Would you not prefer to be with us, if I can make some arrangements for our whole family?"

Rolf was ready to go right then, but he wasn't happy at the thought of leaving his family. If they could find a place for all five of them, that would be preferable. "I'll wait, but I'm going to start working on a move to Canada, too, just as my friend did. My first choice would be for us to go together as a family. My second would be to go to Canada with my friend. But I won't stay here in Happenbach and keep working at something I don't enjoy, with no prospects for it ever getting any better."

They talked for a while longer, with Herman repeatedly assuring Rolf he would do something and Johanna begging her son for more time. After Rolf left, Herman began working more diligently, sending inquiries to country after country with no luck. Finally, in January of 1952, a letter came telling him his efforts had been rewarded.

Herman had some things that needed attending to after work that day, and when he finally made it home, he found Johanna sitting at the table with an unopened envelope in front of her. He looked at it, then at her, saw her expression, and understood their lives might be about to change. He slid a chair out, took his hat and gloves off, unbuttoned his coat, and took a seat. Johanna said nothing. Since she hadn't opened the letter, she couldn't be sure what it said, yet somehow she knew. She slid the envelope across the table, and he read its return address. It was from a church group he'd been told might be of help in getting them to America. He opened the letter, then read it aloud, and when he finished reading it, he laid it down, and the two of them talked about what they would do now that they'd received their answer.

That evening, they called Annelise and Rolf to the house and waited for Georg to come home from working in Abstatt.

When they were all gathered, Rolf asked, "What's going on?"

Herman looked at him and handed him the letter. "We're moving to America."

Rolf scanned the letter, then exclaimed, "All of us?"

"Yes, that is, if the three of you want to go. As you see in the letter, they have a place for us in western Pennsylvania, near a town called Worthington. We'll be living on a farm and helping its owner in exchange for his sponsoring us."

He had a map open on the table and showed them where they'd be going.

Annelise studied the map, wondering if western Pennsylvania was frontier country, with Indians and cowboys. "How did this happen, Father?"

"A church found us a sponsor, and they'll work with the government to arrange our emigration."

"What if it's worse there than it is here?"

"It will be fine, I'm sure."

Johanna had a sense of déjà vu when she heard that. In that split second of memory, she was sitting in the convent in Löhr, with Herman telling her that things would be okay in Poland. Try as she might, it was hard to get past that memory. While she wanted the family to stay together, moving again worried her. Would it be like Poland, or would it be like Strednitz? Or would it be something completely different, and what would that mean? She knew that not taking advantage of this opportunity would divide her family, perhaps forever, so with resignation in her voice, she asked, "How much time do we have?"

"Not much, a few weeks at most. We need to do this, and there's no reason to delay."

"Always with the urgency in these moves—one day we learn we're moving, the next, the move happens!"

Herman shrugged his shoulders and threw up his hands. He'd found the opportunity they wanted. He'd done the best he could. He didn't set the conditions, so once again it was a matter of doing what needed to be done with the hand they'd been dealt.

Georg finally spoke. "I'll repeat Annelise's question: What if we don't like it there?"

"We'll be together, Son. It's a new beginning. It's America, and there'll be other opportunities if we don't like this one."

Annelise wanted to know what kind of agreement they had with the farmer.

"We owe the man one year, and if we choose to do so at the end of that year, we can move on."

Annelise sniffed. "If they'll let us."

"This is America, not Nazi Germany. We'll be able to move."

She still wasn't convinced. "And they won't send us back here?"

"No, Annelise. They won't, and we're all acting as if we won't like it. I've heard it's beautiful there, not unlike some places here in Germany. Germans have settled in Pennsylvania since the 1700s. We may not want to leave once we've spent a year there. We've faced challenges before. We can do this."

The three young Muellers were silent, each of them with their own thoughts.

Herman waited for a moment, then asked, "Well, what do you say?"

Rolf spoke first. "I'm ready. It can only be better than this."

Georg agreed, and Annelise finally gave in. She knew there wasn't much to be gained by staying, and she couldn't picture a life without her family.

So they agreed to leave Happenbach. After all the roads they'd traveled to get there, it hadn't been the worst place to live, and for Georg it held some wonderful boyhood memories, but times were bleak, and America held the best hope—maybe the only hope—for better days.

In February, only a month after that meeting, the Mueller family made their way to Hanau, a town near Frankfurt. Uncle Peter came to wish them well. After losing three of his sons, Peter was nothing like the man he once was. His eyes, once clear and alert, were clouded with grief. He had once stood straight and tall, but he seemed shorter that day, and his shoulders sagged from the weight of all he'd lost. For Herman, saying goodbye to his brother was the hardest part of leaving. It broke his heart seeing Peter looking so beaten down, and the thought that he might never see him again only made it worse.

After they completed their paperwork in Hanau, they went to Bremerhaven and boarded the USS *General Heintzelman*, a ship that was one of hundreds built by Henry Kaiser during the war. Heintzelman and Kaiser—two German names—a good omen they thought. Boarding the *Heintzelman* took them back to 1939 and the day they'd boarded the boat on the Danube. While they had made their own choice this time, that choice had been made necessary because of the actions of the brown-shirted men and their evil masters.

It took ten days to make the Atlantic crossing. Luckily, eight of them were good-weather days, and the sailing was smooth. Two were rough, and most of the passengers spent those days seasick. By the time they approached New York, they were ready to set foot on land again.

✍ 29 ✍

America

March 1952

> The 22nd of March, we saw the Statue of Liberty. On
> the morning of March 23rd, we disembarked at a train
> station. The Salvation Army greeted us with hot coffee
> and donuts and no music. To this day I thank them for
> that. There were no lines to wait in, no papers to fill out,
> no Ellis Island—all [of] that had been done in Hanau.
> All the people left for their destinations. We pretty much
> were left alone for three and a half hours, waiting for a
> train to take us to Pittsburgh, Pennsylvania.
>
> —Excerpt from "A Backward Glance"

The time spent waiting for that train was filled with worry and tension. It was one thing to be on the boat thinking about America. It was an altogether different matter to be sitting on those hard benches with people walking by, looking at them and knowing they were different, and no one speaking German. Herman could see the worry written on the faces of those he loved, and he started to apologize for doing this to them, but it was Johanna who spoke instead. "It will be all right. We're together, and that's the most important thing. We've faced trouble before, and we've made it through. We will again." Herman smiled at hearing words he'd said more than once.

After the train trip across Pennsylvania, they arrived at the station in Pittsburgh, where the farmer's son met them and drove them north to the farm. They took up residence in a small house on the farm. While the farmer's home was not nearly as grand as the big house in Strednitz, their small house was reminiscent of the houses the Czech families lived in.

During the next year, they worked hard to repay the farmer for the opportunity he had given them. But when February 1953 arrived and their one-year obligation had been met, they left the farm and made their way to Columbus, Ohio, where Georg enrolled in high school, finally completing his education.

Eventually, the family would find its way to the heart of America, to a farm in Callaway County, Missouri, not all that far from the river that gave the state its name. And there—after living in Dobrogea, in Poland, in Czechoslovakia, in Happenbach, and then in Pennsylvania and Ohio—they, like so many people from all around the world, found a home in America.

∽ 30 ∾

Callaway County, Missouri

1956

"And you're going to Germany?"

"Yes, Mother, that's where they're sending me."

Johanna looked at Georg, a grown man of twenty, wearing the uniform of an American soldier. She hadn't been excited about his joining the army, but he insisted that he was old enough to enlist, whether she approved or not. She hoped Herman would raise objections and dissuade him, but Herman said nothing, never revealing whether he thought the idea good or bad. But then, Herman was often quiet in those days.

"You'll fly there?"

"Yes, I'll be going with my outfit on a transport."

"Back to Germany as an American soldier. Who could have imagined?"

"When I get some leave I want to go to Altenbamberg and see where our family came from."

Herman smiled upon hearing that. After nearly two centuries, the cycle would be completed—a Mueller near the place Anton had left so long ago. He asked, "And you leave in a few days?"

"Yes, Father. Next week. I'll be there for some time. Make plans to come visit me."

Herman and Johanna looked at each other. Did they have the desire to do that? How would they feel to be back on German soil? They'd lost Detlef and Peter by then, and there were so many horrible memories there.

Herman answered, "Let us think about it. We'd have to find someone to watch things here at the farm, and that isn't always easy to do."

"I won't accept excuses."

"You may have to, Georg. We'll try, though."

Johanna looked at her husband, then at her son, called George by everyone other than his family. He was never a tall boy, but he stood straight, shoulders back, and he looked nice in his uniform. "Be careful of the girls there. They'll see you looking so handsome, and they'll have ideas."

"I can only hope!"

Herman laughed at his son's quip. Georg was his father's son in all respects.

Johanna smiled and asked, "And will there be bicycle trips to Lake Constance?"

Now it was Georg's turn to laugh. She would never let him live that down. "There might be!"

"Such a memory! So much worry."

"I know, but it was a great adventure, and I made it home."

"And then there was another one.

The summer he turned thirteen, Georg had set off on another grand adventure. He'd persuaded his parents to allow him to visit his widowed aunt Elsa and cousin Emma. He pedaled from Happenbach to Miltenberg, having shown his parents the summer before that he could be trusted to make such a long trip alone. Before he left, his mother insisted he send them a telegram as soon as he arrived in Miltenberg, which he did.

Georg enjoyed his time with his relatives. It had been years since he'd seen his aunt and cousin. They talked a little of the past, some about the present, and more of what might lie ahead. Emma was engaged and would be married soon. Her young man came to visit them in the evenings, and they sat outside enjoying the cooling breeze as it swept down the hillsides of the Main River Valley.

At the same time each evening, with dusk approaching, the town became quiet with anticipation. People would stop talking, and whatever traffic there was came to a halt, with people stepping out of their cars to wait for what they knew was about to happen. And then, from the vineyards high above them came the pure sounds of a single trumpet, spilling down the hillside and echoing through the valley. Each piece the young man played seemed better than the one before. He played songs with tempos that lifted the spirits of the people. He played songs so sweet and melancholy people cried.

His music was a gift. After all the tumult and trouble. After the depravity and the destruction. After all the brown shirts, the swastikas, and the Heil Hitlers, such clear, pure music played flawlessly by that young man brought peace to the people of Miltenberg and reminded them of how things could be—should be—while helping to ease the pain and shame of what had been. It was something almost spiritual, something even a thirteen-year-old boy could feel, and Georg carried that memory with him the rest of his life.

While young Georg was gone to Miltenberg, the telegram he'd sent never arrived, causing his parents, especially Johanna, to worry for his safety. She was sure that no news meant something had happened to him, but Herman felt that her sister would have contacted them if Georg hadn't made it to Miltenberg.

Days later, when Georg made it home, Johanna scolded him for not doing as he'd promised. He insisted that he had sent a telegram, but she was sure he'd forgotten and was not being truthful. Two days after he made it back, the telegram arrived. Johanna turned her frustration toward the telegraph company, wondering where the legendary German efficiency had gone.

Even though Georg made it home and the promised telegram did arrive, she let him know there would be no more unaccompanied bicycle trips across Germany. She was too old for such worry.

———

"And true to my word, it was my last trip alone."

"And now you are going back to Germany without us. Please be safe."

"I will."

Johanna looked at her grown son and thought of all he'd been through. She knew he could handle just about anything that came his way. Still she'd miss him and worry about him until the day he returned, just as she had when as a boy he had pedaled across Germany alone.

His year in Germany was a great experience. Being an American soldier who spoke fluent German carried with it many advantages, both professionally and personally, and he made full use of them during his stay. He enjoyed his time there, and he considered making a career of the army.

When he returned to the States after his tour in Germany, he sought an assignment that would have been perfect for him, but the army, as it so often did, went with another man, one less qualified but who most likely spoke English without the hint of a German accent. George left the army soon after that disappointment and began life as an American carpenter, husband, father, and grandfather.

∽ Epilogue ∾

In 1996 George celebrated his sixtieth birthday by traveling to a newly unified Germany with his brother Rolf. They went to the places they'd lived, caught up with their cousins and old friends, and had dinner with two of the Schuster brothers. They also spent some time in the village of Happenbach. The bakehouse was gone by then, but the houses looked much as they had all those years ago, with the people living on the second floor with the barns below. There was one major difference though. They learned that the farmers had banded together to form a co-op, and the co-op decided what crops would be grown on each piece of land. It was a more efficient and profitable way to work, and it allowed the families to survive on those small farms. The thought and organization that went into the planning reminded the brothers of Filip Novák.

With thoughts of Filip and the others, the brothers decided to make the drive to Strednitz to check out the old farm. Their drive took them along the route the family had used to escape at the end of the war. As they drove through Bavaria they talked of how close they'd been to not making it, and how it was their mother as much as anyone who'd gotten them through that horrifying time.

When they made it to Strednitz, they pulled up to the iron gates, newly painted and still looking good, decades after they last saw them. They were open that day, and the brothers could have driven through. Instead they chose to stand at the entrance and look up the hill at the property. The houses on the farm looked well maintained and not that different than when their family had left back in '45. For a moment, George and Rolf felt as if they could walk up that road and find all the people they knew, still going about the day's activities just as it was all those years ago. They realized that five decades later, there would be new people on the farm, and those people might not know who the Muellers were. Even if they knew of them, would they welcome a German family back to Strednitz?

As hard as it was not to go up the hill and see what had changed on the farm, they decided it was better just to take in the view and enjoy the fact that the farm had not only survived but prospered. They accepted that as a proxy for the fate of the families.

Minutes later they got back in their car and began the drive back to Germany. In a few days they would be flying across the Atlantic and returning home.

❧ About the Author ❧

 **Nyle Klinginsmith** earned his Bachelors, Masters, and Educational Doctorate degrees from the University of Missouri-Columbia. During his working years he served as a teacher, counselor, and administrator for the Columbia Public School District. He met his wife, Barb, his first year out of college and they have been together for fifty-two years. They have three sons and three granddaughters.

The Shopkeeper's Family is Klinginsmith's third novel, following *The Brothers Barnhart* and *Harmony Revisited*.

Printed in the USA
CPSIA information can be obtained
at www.ICGtesting.com
LVHW091129230924
791863LV00003B/90